The Brain
Full of Holes

The Brain Full of Holes

Martin Chatterton

LITTLE HARE
www.littleharebooks.com

Little Hare Books
8/21 Mary Street, Surry Hills
NSW 2010 AUSTRALIA

www.littleharebooks.com

National Library of Australia
Cataloguing-in-Publication entry

Author: Chatterton, Martin.

Title: The brain full of holes / author, Martin Chatterton.

Publisher: Surry Hills, N.S.W. : Little Hare Books, 2008.

ISBN: 978 1 921 272 28 8 (pbk.)

Target Audience: For primary school age.

Dewey Number: 823.92

Cover design by Lore Foye
Cover image by permission of Judi Rowe
Cover photograph by Lore Foye
Set in 11/15 pt New Baskerville by Clinton Ellicott
Printed in Australia by Griffin Press, Adelaide

5 4 3 2 1

To Annie, the brain behind The Brain—MC

I

Cheese again.

It was always cheese.

Didn't the Swiss have anything else to put on their sandwiches?

Sheldon McGlone looked at his lunch and shook his head with the air of someone well used to dealing with life's disappointments.

It wasn't that Sheldon really had anything against cheese, or dairy products, or the Swiss for that matter. He'd often enjoyed a tasty cheese sandwich back in Australia. But lately it seemed that all he'd been getting on his school sandwiches was Swiss cheese, chock full of the completely pointless holes that they were so proud of.

Sheldon couldn't see the point of holes in cheese, or any other food. With the possible exception of the bubbles in fizzy drinks, or the bit in the middle of a ring doughnut. Why, he wondered, would anyone go to the trouble of making cheese when a large chunk of the finished article was going to be thin air?

What made things worse was that this sandwich had been made by his mother! Not a Swiss person, but a fellow true-blue Aussie. True, Sheldon's mother, the former Mrs Mary McGlone, having married a Swiss person, was now technically half-Swiss, which made Sheldon McGlone about one-quarter Swiss, or five-sixteenths, or something like that (maths not being Sheldon's strong point). He supposed he'd get used to it eventually, in the same way he was getting used to eating fondue and watching Swiss television.

Sheldon shrugged and took a bite of his sandwich. Lunchtime was lunchtime, after all, and, as cheese sandwiches went, this one wasn't too bad. Looking up with a mouthful of bread and cheese at the ridiculously beautiful mountains, he had to admit that, from this angle, Switzerland wasn't half bad, either.

It was another effortlessly sensational Alpine day, one of an odd series that had been turning up again and again recently, despite it being officially winter. Probably global warming, thought Sheldon. Most things were, these days. Whatever it was, it felt pretty good. The blue sky stretched itself across the snow-capped mountains and Sheldon snorted up another lungful of air crisper than a jumbo bag of extra-crispy, spearmint-flavoured crisps. The air was very different to the slow-moving, chunky sort of air he'd left behind in Farrago Bay. Not that the Aussie air was polluted—it was simply that this Alpine stuff felt like it had been freshly made every morning just for him. It was so good that, from time to time, Sheldon even felt the urge to have a bit of a yodel. There was something about the echoing valleys between the Alps, and the springy, flower-strewn meadows, that lent itself to yodelling. Of course, Sheldon knew he'd never give in to the temptation.

Beside Sheldon at the school lunch table, his step-brother, best friend, and self-styled World's Greatest

Detective, Theophilus Nero Hercule Sherlock Wimsey Father Brown Marlowe Spade Christie Edgar Allen Brain, adjusted his battered spectacles, lifted the corner of his identical sandwich with the end of his unlit pipe and peered suspiciously inside.

'Remarkable,' he said.

'I know!' said Sheldon shaking his head from side to side. 'Swiss cheese. Again!'

'Ah,' said The Brain. 'That wasn't quite what … never mind.'

The Brain was always doing things like that. Just when you thought you knew what he was thinking, he'd surprise you by revealing that he was, in fact, thinking about something entirely different. Sheldon looked at The Brain— almost everyone called him that—and not for the first time since they'd arrived in Switzerland, Sheldon thought about what a strange, complicated journey it had been to end up here, related to this rather odd-looking individual.

The first thing you noticed about The Brain was the size of his head. It wasn't so big that it made people form a baying mob armed with pitchforks and flaming torches intent on stringing him up from the nearest tower, but it was definitely on the sizeable side. And anyone who knew The Brain knew that the reason he needed a head that size, was that a normal-sized head simply would not have been large enough to contain the astonishing amount of fizzing little grey cells that were stuffed in there.

Perched on top of The Brain's head was a thatch of spiky black hair cut with no style. It had no style because The Brain, quite frankly, usually had more important things to think about than hair care. Below his hair, in the place you'd expect to find it, was The Brain's face. Thick-rimmed glasses that enlarged his piercingly intelligent eyes sat on a small nose. When required, he could turn those eyes on someone in a way that made them feel like an insignificant bug. Sheldon had been on the receiving end more than a few times. The Brain wasn't tall but could not be described as short. He was skinny, with a wiry frame that Sheldon's mother (The Brain's new stepmother) was doing her best to pad out.

'There's nothing of you,' she'd say, slopping out another gigantic plateful of grey meat and soggy potatoes. 'You need some flesh on those bones or you'll fade away!'

The Brain would thank her politely, pretend to eat, and never gain an ounce. Whether this was due to Mrs McGlone-Schnurrbart's staggeringly revolting cooking, or to The Brain's digestive system, was hard to tell.

Sheldon had almost finished his sandwich.

'You know, if this was a book, someone would pop up and explain exactly how we got here.'

'Hmm?' said The Brain absent-mindedly. His attention still seemed to be on the contents of the Swiss cheese sandwich.

'I said, if this was a book, someone would tell everyone about us solving the case back in Farrago Bay ...'

'Yes, old boy,' said The Brain, '*if* this was a book, that would almost certainly be the case, but I'm afraid real life's not like that. Fascinating as it is, the story of how we thwarted the evil machinations of the evil Dr Dirk Unsinn will have to remain our secret. No-one will "pop up", as you say.'

'I suppose you're right,' said Sheldon.

Sheldon concentrated on his sandwich, then realised that The Brain was speaking again. 'What? Hmm?' said Sheldon.

'The cheese sandwiches, dear boy.'

'What about the cheese sandwiches?'

Was The Brain still droning on about those cheese sandwiches? Sometimes he was like a dog with a bone.

'Holes,' said The Brain. 'That's what about them.'

Sheldon shrugged. 'So what?' he said. 'Swiss cheese is full of holes. That's the whole point of Swiss cheese. Hey? Did you see what I did there? You said "holes" and I said "whole"—'

'Yes, very good, Sheldon. Most amusing.'

'Don't sulk,' said Sheldon. 'What were you saying about the holes?'

'They've gone,' said The Brain.

'Gone? What do you mean "gone"? A hole isn't really there in the first place, is it? How can it go?'

'Observe,' said The Brain, opening his sandwich and thrusting it under Sheldon's nose. 'My sandwich has cheese, as you can see. Plenty of cheese, in fact. A positive abundance of the stuff. Rather more than I prefer, to be perfectly honest. But as must be plain, there is a complete absence of holes. An absence of absences, you might say. Of my holes there is no sign. *Rien de holes. Keine Bohrungen.*'

The Brain was right.

The holes had completely disappeared.

Still, they *were* just holes. Sheldon found he couldn't work up very much excitement about their disappearance.

'Holes, shmoles, what does it matter? Probably just a dud batch of cheese Mum used or something. Who cares?'

The Brain paused. 'You do not think it is of interest, this lack of holes? In my humble opinion, this is a most singular occurrence and one that I am determined to investigate until I am satisfied with the outcome. As far as this being a "dud" batch, I can assure you of this: the cheese from which this particular sandwich has been made was placed in the refrigerator yesterday evening. I observed that it had, at that time, a full complement of holes. That, dear boy, is why the current hole-free situation is so deuced odd.'

Sheldon looked at his own sandwich with more interest. If what The Brain said was true, then it *was* a bit odd that the holes had somehow disappeared overnight. He peeled back the top layer of bread and checked his own sandwich.

No holes.

'Couldn't it just be a coincidence?' said Sheldon. 'Maybe Mum switched cheeses last night after we went to bed?'

The Brain nodded. Sheldon could tell it was the sort of nod that, when translated, meant 'I'm nodding, but not because I agree with you, but to suggest that you are, in fact, an idiot.'

Sheldon gave up. Trying to figure out what The Brain was talking about often made his head hurt. He picked up his can of Floop, the repulsive home-brand version of Coke that his mother insisted on buying, and took a slurp.

'Typical,' he said, looking at the can in disgust. 'Flat as a pancake.'

The Brain looked up, his eyes bright.

'Flat you say? May I?'

Sheldon reluctantly handed him the Floop. Flat or not, it was still the only one he had.

The Brain took a pull on the can and screwed up his face.

'A truly nauseating concoction. But you are quite correct, it is quite devoid of carbonation.'

Sheldon looked blank.

'No bubbles,' explained The Brain. 'Interesting.'

Sheldon grabbed back the can and drained it in one greedy gulp.

'Yeah,' he said, burping. 'Very interesting. You got any more Floop? One with bubbles?'

The Brain poured steaming Earl Grey tea from a silver thermos flask into the monogrammed, fine bone-china teacup he brought to school every day.

'Good grief, no,' he said, stirring the tea with a gleaming silver teaspoon. 'One has one's standards, old boy.'

He sipped his tea thoughtfully, picked up his sandwich once again and inspected it closely.

Sheldon shook his head sadly. The Brain was a certified genius (he had the certificate on his bedroom wall to prove it), but sometimes Sheldon had to wonder if his stepbrother was, perhaps, a few sandwiches short of the full picnic. Even if they were Swiss cheese sandwiches.

Holes or no holes, bubbles or no bubbles, there seemed to be little chance of solving the puzzle this lunchtime. Once that bell sounded for the afternoon, class work started immediately. This was Switzerland after all.

Sheldon grabbed The Brain's sandwich.

'If you're not going to eat that, do you mind if I have it?

Thanks.' Without waiting for a reply, he crammed it into his mouth.

'Stop!' yelled The Brain. 'You're eating the evidence!'

Too late. The bell sounded and Switzerland sprang back into action.

2

It didn't take long for the twins to find him again. Sheldon was just finishing putting some books back in his school locker when they pounced.

'Shel-*don*,' said one of them, a boy called Erich or Franck, Sheldon could never tell which. He had the usual look on his face, somewhere between a smirk and a sneer.

'Shel-*don*,' said the other twin in a mocking singsong voice. 'Funny name, Shel-*don*. Although really it should be more like Shel-*don't*.'

'As in, Shel-*don't* do so well in Super Hard Maths. Is that what you mean, Franck?' said Erich.

'Yes, Erich, that's correct,' said Franck. 'And Shel-*don't* do so well in Quantum Physics Theory.'

'In fact, it's something of a miracle you can tie your own shoes, isn't it, Shel-*don't*?' said Erich. 'Or does Mummy do them for you? Hmm?'

They'd been like this ever since Sheldon had arrived at the school, but he wasn't too worried. Compared to Fergus Feebley, Sheldon's chief bully back in Australia, the twins were a pushover. Even Sheldon, who knew he'd never make a fighter, fancied his chances against the twins. They were almost blind for one thing. Sheldon reckoned that their white canes would slow them up a bit if it came down to a straight fight.

He fastened his locker and turned round.

'All done?' he said. 'Had the anti-Sheldon fix for the day?'

The twins appeared to be taking Sheldon's question seriously. There was a brief silence before they nodded.

'Yes,' they said in unison. 'That will be all for the moment Shel-*don't*.'

Erich and Franck turned as one and walked slowly down the corridor, their white sticks tap-tapping against the tiles. Sheldon watched them, his face a blank. He had hoped that in Switzerland he'd be free from the idiot brigade that had made his classroom life difficult in Farrago Bay.

So much for that theory.

There was, however, one important difference between the Sheldon McGlone who had been tormented in Australia and the new, improved Sheldon model currently on the market in Switzerland. That difference was in his reaction to the bullies. After all the things he'd been through in The Case of the Missing Leg, he was less of an easy target. If he thought about it (which he didn't very often, as he generally found that too much thinking made the back of his head hurt), once you'd been shot, handled a four metre crocodile, helped defeat an evil scientist and saved the world from an outbreak of mass stupidity, a couple of visually impaired boneheads weren't going to make you lose much sleep.

Sheldon picked up his school bag and hurried down the corridor with a small smile on his face. This afternoon's lesson was Unarmed Combat 101 and he couldn't wait to get there.

*

Outwardly, the Ecole Suisse Speciale looked like any other school. It clung to the side of a long ridge road, at the end of a winding series of white-knuckle hairpin bends that looped terrifyingly up the side of the mountain. If anyone took the trouble to think about it—which no-one ever seemed to—it was a rather odd place for a school; remote, forbidding, unwelcoming.

Which was exactly why the Swiss Scientific SWAT Unit had picked that spot.

It had been purpose-built as a training school for the top secret SSSU, the main headquarters of which spread, octopus-like, in an underground complex cut below the school. Even Sheldon, who didn't consider himself much of an observer, had noticed that if there was one thing that Switzerland had plenty of it was mountains. In fact, they had more than was strictly comfortable in what was, after all, a small country. You couldn't move anywhere in Switzerland without bumping into an alp or two. Naturally, with all these mountains clogging up the place, whenever the Swiss decided to build something, they almost always had to tunnel out a bit of an alp and bung the structure underneath. The entire school would have probably been underground if it wasn't for the government fussily insisting on pupils having access to daylight.

Students at the Ecole were divided into two groups— those who knew about the school's secret SSSU training program, and those who didn't. The students who were unaware of the top-secret organisation beneath their feet were known by the SSSU students as 'civilians'.

Sheldon himself, although obviously not a civilian,

didn't quite know where he fitted into the whole SSSU set-up.

At school, he struggled with the more advanced scientific lessons and couldn't help feeling that it might only have been his relationship with the respected Captain Schnurrbart that enabled him to get into the SSSU program. In Farrago Bay, Sheldon had not been an A-grade student, and his friendship with The Brain hadn't worked any sudden miracles in that department. Unless you counted the time he'd fallen into the Genius Machine and become super-intelligent for about five minutes. Sheldon sometimes thought fondly of those five minutes and wished that The Brain hadn't been so quick to reverse the process.

Sheldon snapped out of his daydream as he reached the entrance to the SSSU section of the school, which was sealed from prying eyes by a large steel security door cleverly disguised as the entrance to a storage shed. After a quick check to make sure there were no civilians around, he produced a plastic swipe card and slid it through the card reader set into the wall. With an almost undetectable hum, the door rolled open on its expertly engineered runners.

Sheldon stepped into a large lift and pressed a button. With a soft hum, the lift descended underground. After a few seconds, it stopped and the doors opened out into the huge natural cavern that had first attracted the school architects to this particular site. It meant that the secret SSSU training area could sit below the regular school in complete secrecy. Nothing would show up on satellite images of the work going on at SSSU.

The space had the appearance of a gigantic gymnasium—

a vast, high-ceilinged room set into the solid rock that contained basketball courts, gym equipment, climbing ropes, fight mats and a full-scale weapons training environment. This last section, known by all SSSU students as 'The Street', was just that: a short section of what appeared to be a road, complete with buildings, signs, cars and booby traps. The Street was where SSSU students learned how to cope with all kinds of lethal attack.

A red 'class in action' sign above the main entrance warned other students not to enter The Street under any circumstances. A smart-alec student called Victor Vidic had entered it while a class was in action three years ago and there had been an unfortunate incident with a flame thrower.

A blue plaque on the wall outside the entrance to The Street was all that remained to remind people of Victor. It had become a habit for students to touch Victor's plaque for luck. Victor's name was almost invisible now, worn away by years of superstitious touching.

A senior class was in The Street now, their instructor hovering above the action on a mobile, magnetically powered, hover scooter. He observed and directed the exercise, talking quietly into a mouthpiece that Sheldon knew linked him to each student via hi-tech speakers in their helmets. The class was dressed in black, the school colour. Each student moved cautiously as he or she came under attack from the usual: guns, bombs, man-eating tigers and the like. Sheldon could feel the explosions through the thick, soundproof glass. The students dodged high-powered bullets that slammed viciously into the scarred concrete as they dived for cover.

As it was a senior class, they were using live ammunition. Sheldon flinched as a round of high velocity tracer fire bounced off the glass metres from him, even though the glass could withstand a direct hit from a tank. This had been demonstrated to Sheldon's class a few months earlier, when Sheldon had been 'volunteered' to stand directly in front of the glass as the tank blasted away. Quite a memorable day, that one.

Reluctantly Sheldon turned away from The Street as the first three tigers were released. He hurried towards the Unarmed Combat class that was taking place in the centre of the gym on a section of padded mats.

'Good afternoon Sheldon,' said the instructor, Miss Urtl, who, in addition to her role as the Ecole's unarmed combat teacher, also taught cookery. 'Good of you to join us.' She tapped her small foot impatiently.

'Sorry, Miss Urtl,' mumbled Sheldon.

Miss Urtl, known to SSSU students as 'Urtl the Turtle'— although never, *ever* to her face—was a short, dumpy woman, with a fondness for shapeless brown cardigans and Toblerone chocolate. She looked like everyone's favourite sweet-natured granny, but with one vital difference: unlike most people's grandmothers, Miss Urtl knew twenty-seven different ways to kill someone with a straw, and eighty-six ways of subduing a wild animal using only her little finger. She was an expert in all forms of unarmed combat with a particular fondness for a blend of capoeira, the deadly Brazilian street-fighting discipline, and Ecky Thump, the ancient and almost extinct Yorkshire martial art. Many a SSSU recruit had made the mistake of underestimating the formidable Miss Urtl, only to wake up face down on the fight mat asking for his mummy and wondering why his arm was at a funny angle.

There was one particular piece of information about Miss Urtl that was troubling Sheldon at that moment. She did not like people being late for class.

As she often said, if you're attacked down some dark alley one night, the attacker isn't going to wait around for *you* to be late, is he? Sheldon wasn't sure that what she said made any kind of sense, but he knew better than to question her wisdom. He also knew that being late meant he was sure to be on the pointy end of Miss Urtl's skills.

The Brain was sitting cross-legged on the opposite side of the mat, one of a line of sixteen students. He raised his eyebrows in a question and tapped his watch with a bony finger. Sheldon held up two fingers and The Brain nodded. The twins. Say no more.

Miss Urtl removed her brown cardigan, hooked it on the back of a nearby chair and walked into the exact centre of the mat. She was a few centimetres shorter than Sheldon and peered up at him through a pair of spectacles balanced on her little blob of a nose.

'Very well, now we have the attention of the *full* class we can begin. Today we're going to learn how to deal with an attack from behind. We need a volunteer. Thank you, Sheldon, so kind. Step forward and try to grab my throat. Don't be shy, now; really make a lunge.'

Sheldon knew not to argue. In her class, Miss Urtl's word was law. Without much enthusiasm, he slid cautiously onto the mat and walked towards her, as confident as someone following a hungry bear into a dark cave. Which is to say, not very. Sheldon didn't need to be told that he was in trouble. Armpit deep, smelly doo-doo type trouble.

Miss Urtl was standing, seemingly defenceless, her small arms down by her side, looking every inch the bewildered old lady. Sheldon shuffled cautiously towards her. As he drew nearer, she held up her hand and pointed to her shoelace which was undone. Holding out a palm to ask him to wait, she bent down and began to fasten it.

Sheldon's heart skipped a beat. This was his chance! Didn't Miss Urtl always tell them not to hesitate, to take advantage of any error by your opponent, to exploit any weakness no matter how underhand it may seem? Maybe this was her big mistake. Sheldon reached out to grab her. Just goes to show, he thought, the old dear was losing her touch, getting slopp—

There was a rapid blur of movement, as graceful and deadly as a cobra, and before Sheldon could say so much as 'oof', Miss Urtl flipped him casually over her head.

'BY-ECK-LAD!' yelled Miss Urtl, the familiar Ecky Thump war cry echoing off the cavern roof. Sheldon slammed, back first, into the padding with a sickening *whump* that expelled every atom of breath from his lungs. Miss Urtl picked a stray thread of wool from her cardigan and looked at Sheldon who was lying on his back gasping.

'Very good, young man,' she said. 'You make a perfect volunteer. So *wonderfully* trusting! Restores my faith in human nature, seeing your innocent little puppy dog face coming towards me. Now, let's go over it again. And this time, don't let yourself get fooled by simple misdirection.

I mean, did you really think that I would ever leave a shoelace untied in a combat situation?'

Sheldon felt he may never be able to speak again. He'd have to learn how to breathe before he could think about doing anything as ambitious as speaking.

It was going to be one of those days.

3

Schnarchen is, at first, second, third, and even fourth glance, a perfectly ordinary Swiss mountain village exactly like so many others dotted prettily around the Alps. A few main streets winding up and down, the solid wooden houses neat and well cared for. There's a general feeling of contentment and permanence about the place, as if it has always been sleepy and peaceful and that's just how the residents like it, thank you very much. From the point of view of the Schnurrbart-McGlones, who chose Schnarchen as their home, it couldn't be better placed, sitting only ten kilometres east of SSSU headquarters, with Lucce only twenty kilometres to the south.

Just before nine o'clock on a Saturday evening, Schnarchen was as silent as a librarian's grave. A blanket of snow lay thick on the ground. The morning may have been sunny and warm, but right now it felt very much like mid-winter. The snow fell steadily: thick saucer-sized flakes drifting silently out of the darkness and deadening Schnarchen's few night noises to nothing.

Almost everyone in town had turned in for the night, but, here and there, warm orange light glowed invitingly through the triple-glazed windows, indicating some wild-living types who'd decided to stay up past nine.

Behind one of those windows, Sheldon's mother, Mary,

looked glumly into the back garden where her new husband was leaping, nude, into a large snow drift. He briskly rubbed snow up and down his muscular frame before dropping to the ground and doing fifty press-ups. It was Captain Schnurrbart's habit to spend some time each evening practising the almost forgotten Swiss martial art of Slaadstaat which, for some reason, required a nude roll in the snow after each session. What would happen when the summer came and the snow departed, Mary couldn't imagine. Possibly the Captain would spend some time sitting chest deep in the freezer in the basement. He was a good man, but this Switzerland business was going to take some getting used to.

As she regarded the Captain's snow-flecked pink backside sticking up out of the snow, she reached automatically for a cigarette. Then she remembered with a stab of irritation that, through her husband's persuasion, she'd given up. Reluctantly, she turned her attention to the *Teach Yourself German* language book open in front of her. She hadn't got past the opening chapter. Switzerland, she found, much to her frustration, used a mixture of French and German, along with a fair dollop of Italian and even a few spicy local Romansh and mountain dialects, the languages shifting mysteriously as you moved across the country. It was downright sneaky, if you asked Mary. She was trying hard, but languages were proving not to be her strong point.

'Flamin' book!' she muttered.

Mary wouldn't have bothered with foreign languages if it hadn't been that her ignorance was interfering with her favourite pastime: watching quite astonishingly large amounts of television. Some of the programs were in English with French or German subtitles, but most were in some foreign language or other.

She looked up as the cuckoo clock sounded nine. The bird had an irritating, high-pitched chirp that Mary had often thought about silencing. Instead, she stalked upstairs to have a bath.

Sheldon watched her go. He hoped she'd settle into the new life soon. It was one thing for him to be homesick—he was only thirteen, after all—but wasn't his mum supposed to comfort him? He knew she missed Sean, Sheldon's older and dumber brother, although exactly why that would be the case was a complete mystery to Sheldon. He regarded Sean as a step up from a slug: a particularly low-life slug. Sean had remained in Farrago Bay to carve out an exciting career as a part-time surfer, part-time pizza delivery guy and (according to Sheldon), full-time bonehead.

Sheldon's mum, who was still coming to grips with the time difference, phoned Sean often, waking him at odd hours of the night. Sheldon couldn't imagine what she found to discuss with Sean. Soap opera plots most likely.

Sheldon turned to the television, picked up the remote and began clicking. The screen flickered uncertainly and a fuzzy picture came into view. It showed a man with what looked like a shiny dead possum taped to his head, warbling a love song to a woman in a tight, glittery, purple catsuit. Behind the pair, a small orchestra chimed in with sugary strings as the song creaked towards its grisly climax.

Sheldon shuddered and pressed another channel. Again the screen flickered and the baldy warbler popped up once more. Irritated, Sheldon jabbed his finger down on the remote.

Flick. Baldy warbler.

Flick. Baldy warbler.

Flick. Each channel seemed to be showing the same show.

'Weird,' mumbled Sheldon. He dropped the remote and settled back. TV was TV, after all, and Sheldon needed a fix. The meal his mother had prepared earlier sat like a bad-tempered troll in his stomach, daring him to move off the couch. Never one to deliberately take risks, Sheldon sank into the cushions and let Swiss TV wash over him.

The show, called *Eurovisionara Dong Ding!* or some such rubbish, was a song competition between European nations. Strangely, this also included some countries that were not in Europe. It was being broadcast live from Geneva. The audience and the various presenters seemed excited to the point of stupidity by the whole shebang. Sheldon decided it was the cheesiest thing he'd ever seen. It was the essence of cheese; a steaming pile of television gorgonzola.

Believe it or not, it was worse than Australian TV.

'I don't think much of the Lithuanian entry,' said Sheldon after two rappers from Vilnius had tested his TV-watching nerve to the very limits. 'I reckon the Latvians will nail this one.'

The Latvian *Eurovisionara* entry consisted of a man wearing a spacesuit and an expression of grim determination. He kept smacking himself on the head with a tin tray and screeching the word 'Shmek' over and over. It was, depending on how you looked at it, either the funniest thing ever, or total manure. Sheldon was still deciding which camp his opinion fell into as the song got faster and faster, louder and louder. The Latvian singer threw down his tray theatrically as the performance built to a dramatic climax. He picked up a trumpet, sucked up a mighty breath and blew hard into the mouthpiece.

A small, sad, strangled note leaked pathetically out of the end of the instrument. It sounded like a leaky balloon.

Brrrrpt!

The Latvian looked into the trumpet, puzzled. He shook it and put it to his lips once more.

Brrrrpt! Neeept! Parp!

The Latvian shook his head, threw the trumpet to the floor and stalked off the stage, his *Eurovisionara* hopes in tatters. An uncomfortable silence from the Geneva audience was broken by an agitated announcer bounding onto the stage to cover the problem.

'Hmm,' hummed Sheldon. 'What was *that* all about?'

The Brain looked up from the complex jumble of wires, lights and computer equipment he'd assembled on the dining room table and scratched his chin thoughtfully.

'Interesting,' he murmured before turning back to the table.

Sheldon, his curiosity tweaked by The Brain's new experiment, wandered over.

'What's all this?'

The Brain glanced up before returning his gaze to a digital monitor.

'It's a little spectron image analyser I put together from a few odds and ends. I wanted a closer look at that cheese— at the particle level. I'm calling it a "Cheesotron".'

Sheldon rolled his eyes.

'Are you still banging on about that cheese? I thought you were doing something, y'know, important.'

'As a matter of fact—' began The Brain, when he was interrupted by a loud buzz. Someone was at the door.

'I wonder who that is?' muttered Sheldon. 'It's a stinker of a night outside.'

The Brain looked up.

'I predict our caller is a worried young female, aged perhaps fourteen, with blonde hair. She is wearing a black North Face ski jacket and a red fleece hat.'

'My God, Brain!' gasped Sheldon. The Brain's powers of detection never failed to impress him, but this was truly amazing. 'That was incredible! How did you do that?'

'I have told you before, dear boy, my methods, once revealed, appear to be far from miraculous.'

'Yes, I know, but … still! How on earth did you deduce all that?'

'I can see her on the door monitoring camera.'

He nodded towards a small screen mounted above the fridge. It displayed a clear video image of the visitor.

'Ah,' said Sheldon, who had completely forgotten about the security measures Captain Schnurrbart had installed around the house.

'I told you you'd be disappointed.'

The Brain pressed a button on an electronic pad mounted on the wall and the downstairs door opened to admit the visitor.

'I think she looks harmless enough, don't you?' said The Brain. 'Besides, I have an idea that this will perhaps be even more interesting than examining the remains of my cheese sandwich. I think we'll see our visitor in our rooms, Sheldon. This may be a confidential matter.'

Moments later the visitor walked in, brushing snow from her shoulders. She removed her hat, shivered, and shook out her long blonde hair.

Sheldon goggled. He could have sworn her hair tumbled out in slow motion, and was accompanied by a chorus of heavenly harp players twanging away fit to bust. The new arrival stepped into the table lamp's glow and Sheldon felt something shift in the pit of his stomach. He was pretty sure it wasn't the remains of his dinner. He opened and closed his mouth. And then, as if impersonating a goldfish, repeated the process.

The Brain rolled his eyes before holding out a hand to greet the visitor.

'*Guten Abend,*' said The Brain. '*Kommen Sie bitte herein und warmen Sie sich. Peut-etre vous parleriez plutot francais?* Or will English be acceptable?'

The visitor nodded. 'Good evening,' she said in a soft, lightly accented voice. 'English will be fine.'

'Very well,' said The Brain. 'This way, please. I think we'll be more comfortable in private.'

He led her past the Cheesotron into the area of the house set aside for Sheldon and The Brain's use. Their bed-rooms were situated at the end of a long, narrow, L-shaped room that wrapped around the back of the house. The visitor looked round curiously.

Books were everywhere; spilling from shelves, stacked in random teetering towers across the room, on chairs, under tables. A pool table at one end had been almost entirely covered with a complicated scientific experiment featuring burbling test tubes, glass flasks of noxious substances and a complex spaghetti of tubes and piping. It looked impressive, but was in fact an effort to produce a version of a popular Australian snack spread. Sheldon hadn't been able to find a supply in Switzerland and the Brain had offered to whip up a batch from some old socks and belly-button fluff. So far, despite one or two unfortunate accidental poisonings, the results had been encouraging.

A gigantic grandfather clock stood in a shadowy corner, topped by a stuffed vulture, its single remaining glass eye glittering in the firelight from the log fire. Naturally, this being Switzerland, the logs were made of carbon composite and the flame was clean-burning natural gas, but the effect was pretty much the same as the real thing. The fire burned in an oversized fireplace crowned by a heavy marble mantle on which stood a bewildering variety of objects. Jostling for space, in no particular order, were an antique snuff box, an electric violin, a slim black laptop, a jar of what looked like pickled lizard skeletons, several top hats piled on top of one another, a lava lamp, pieces of a broken surfboard, a Geiger counter, lengths of rubber tubing, a second stuffed vulture and a smaller stuffed ocelot posed as if engaged in deadly combat.

At either side of the fire, two battered wing-backed chairs faced inwards, the red leather gleaming in the firelight. On the chair used mostly by The Brain, the leather was spotted and stained here and there with chemical spills from various experiments. Sheldon's chair was covered in discarded toffee wrappers, music magazines, and what looked like a pet cat but was, in fact, a ratty Russian fur hat he had been wearing in bed to keep his ears warm. He hurriedly scooped up the debris and threw the hat, toffee wrappers and magazines behind a large cardboard cut-out of an American rap performer.

The Brain turned to the new arrival.

'Please take a seat,' he said. 'It is a cold night and I am sure you will be more comfortable closer to the fire. Sheldon, please be so good as to take our visitor's coat and hat. This is my associate, Sheldon McGlone.'

The girl flicked a grateful glance at Sheldon.

Close up, her green eyes reminded him of high alpine meadows under the merest sprinkling of fresh spring snow, and her hair of a cascade of hand-spun golden silk ...

'Thank you,' she said.

'*Hurn-unch, gnn!*' Sheldon snorted, his reddening face contorted into what he imagined was a welcoming smile, but which, in fact, made him look as though he was trying to eat a harmonica. His tongue appeared to be glued to the roof of his mouth.

'Yes,' said The Brain. 'Very smooth, Sheldon. Now I am sure our visitor could use a hot drink. She has come a long way to be here tonight with, if I'm not mistaken, a ticklish problem concerning a family member. She has also agonised for some cold minutes outside in the cold before deciding to ring our doorbell.'

'No problem,' said Sheldon. He zipped out to the kitchen for some hot chocolate.

'How did you know all that information about me,' said

the visitor coolly, her eyes narrowing. 'I mean, it's all true. I *have* come a long way and I did wait before ringing the bell. And this *is* about my family. My father. But how . . .?'

The Brain picked up his unlit pipe and settled comfortably back in his chair.

'It is of little consequence and extremely simple. Poking from your coat pocket is the edge of a train ticket showing the distinctive orange print of the Zurich train system which places the start of your journey there: no small distance on a night such as this. The fact that you have apparently made the journey at this late hour (for Switzerland) indicates some mental anguish; the sort usually associated with family or loved ones in trouble. And, forgive me for saying this, but your expression is not a happy one; it betrays some high emotions in recent days. As for the time spent outside, that is explained easily enough: the distance between the train station and this house is only two minutes walk, but the amount of snow that clung to your hat told me you had spent more than a few minutes lingering in the street before taking the decision to consult me. It is a decision I am sure you will not regret and one that I am most curious about. Already there are aspects of your case that are of interest.'

The girl allowed herself a small smile.

'I have come to the right place, then,' she said. 'The internet rumours are true? You *are* the world's greatest detective?'

The Brain nodded. 'Modesty is much over-rated don't you think?' he said briskly. 'It saves so much time when one knows what one is capable of. Now, let us not waste any more time. Your problem: please tell us your story and omit nothing, absolutely nothing, I implore you! Pray let me decide what is and isn't relevant.'

The Brain placed the tips of his fingers together and closed his eyes as if meditating.

Sheldon returned with the hot chocolate. He handed it to the girl and pulled up a third chair. Outside, the wind howled through the empty streets of Schnarchen. The three of them could have been the only people in the world at that moment. Their visitor brushed a stray blonde curl from her forehead and began her story.

'My name is Helga. Helga Poom of the Zurich Pooms. You will not have heard of our family, we are not rich or famous or glamorous in any way.'

Sheldon looked as though he was going to disagree with Helga's last statement but he contented himself with making a sound like a trained seal asking for another fish.

'The problem I have is my father, Pieter. He, well . . . the flat truth of it is that he's disappeared. He's a truck driver. He was last seen on Wednesday afternoon setting off from Lucce. He was heading south. As you may know, the route south from Lucce passes through the Furcht tunnel. A driver who knows my father passed my father as he entered the tunnel. He was travelling in the opposite direction. He remembers waving to him . . . but my father doesn't seem to have come out the other side.'

The Brain opened his eyes.

'Most interesting,' he murmured. 'The Furcht you say?'

Helga nodded.

'I know it,' said The Brain. 'It's not too far (more or less side by side, in fact) from the new LURV complex. The

Lucce Ultra Radiation Venture. It's only been operational for a few months. The Captain's been there recently to check security measures. It is a most *interesting* place. I have been keeping my eye on it for some time.'

'What is it?' asked Sheldon.

'You've heard of CERN, the particle accelerator laboratory near Geneva? No? Well CERN is, or was until LURV came along, the world's largest particle accelerator. LURV is a huge thing, more than ten kilometres long. Over six thousand scientists from all over the world conduct experiments there. The new accelerator is on a site not far from Lucce.'

'Yes, yes,' said Sheldon, 'but what, exactly, does a particle accelerator do?'

The Brain opened his mouth, but it was Helga Poom who spoke.

'A particle accelerator,' she said, 'accelerates particles at extremely high speeds controlled by powerful magnetic fields by firing them round a gigantic circular tunnel, and then smashes them into objects to see what happens.'

Sheldon blinked.

'Put simply, the particle accelerator is an attempt to find out more about the stuff that makes up the entire universe; me, you, the mountains, the air we breathe, the galaxies . . . everything.'

'Oh,' said Sheldon, blinking again. 'I see.' Although he didn't, not quite.

'Most illuminating, Miss Poom,' said The Brain. 'I had no idea you were an expert.'

'Oh no, not really,' said Helga. 'Science is a passion of mine, that's all.'

The Brain sat back in his chair.

'You will pardon me for this observation but you hardly seem like the typical daughter of a truck driver.'

Helga nodded. 'I am an only child, Herr Brain ...'

Sheldon sniggered and she broke off.

'What's so funny, Sheldon?' asked The Brain.

'Oh, nothing. Just that she—I mean Helga—said "Herr Brain". *Harebrain*, get it?'

'Most amusing,' said The Brain. 'Please continue, Miss Poom.'

'Well, yes, as I was saying, my father denies me nothing, including the very best education that money can buy. Ever since my mother died he has devoted his life to me. Truck driver he may be but, thanks to him, I am a proud student at The Alpine Ladies College of Zurich.'

The Brain whistled softly. The Alpine Ladies College was the finest, most expensive school in Switzerland and, therefore, the planet.

'It is difficult for him,' she said. 'He makes ... sacrifices.'

'What, like goats and stuff?' Sheldon blurted out.

Helga stared at him. Not for the first time, Sheldon wished that his mouth would check with his brain before coming out with things like that.

'I don't think it's likely that Miss Poom's father sacrifices goats, Sheldon. Or hens, or pigs or humans, for that matter. She simply means he makes personal sacrifices in order to afford her school fees.'

Sheldon nodded miserably. This talking-to-girls business was harder than it looked.

'Please, Miss Poom, continue your story.'

'Well, that's about it,' said Helga, glancing in Sheldon's direction, as if she expected him to start howling or something equally loopy. 'I called the truck company, and it turns out my father didn't show up at his drop-off point. They were quite rude, to be honest; kept insinuating he may have taken off and sold the truck or its contents. But my father's not like that! He would never have just left me without a word. And he is *not* a thief.'

Tears came to her eyes, and Sheldon leaned forward to offer her a box of tissues.

'Thank you,' said Helga.

'*Nngg-tchagnnn,*' said Sheldon, his face the colour of a red bell pepper.

'The police?' said The Brain impatiently.

'Horrid!' said Helga, shuddering. 'They were so rude to me. Kept saying that maybe my father wanted to sell the truck, maybe he had gambling problems, that sort of thing. All nasty lies and nonsense!'

'Is there anything else you can think of, Miss Poom?'

Helga thought for a moment and wrinkled her perfect little nose.

'No,' she said. 'I think that's everything.'

The Brain rose to his feet and paced briskly back and forward in front of the fire. His voice took on a business-like tone.

'So it is down to us, my dear,' he said. 'We must find your father for you. It is as simple as that. Now I have one or two further questions.'

'Anything.'

The Brain pointed his pipe at Helga and fixed her with

a piercing stare. Sheldon remembered how disconcerting he'd found that look the first time he'd seen it, but Helga did not seem to notice. In fact, despite her warm expression, she had something rather steely about her own eyes. Sheldon could easily imagine her giving The Brain a run for his money. Sheldon focussed his attention back on the conversation. The Brain was about to ask the first important question of the investigation. An exciting moment.

'His sandwiches. What sort of sandwiches did he take with him on Tuesday?'

Sheldon and Helga stared at The Brain.

'Um, he had ham, I think,' said Helga.

'Not cheese?' said The Brain. 'You are sure it wasn't Swiss cheese?'

'Yes. I mean, no, it wasn't Swiss cheese. I'm sure. But what does that have to do with—'

The Brain waved away Helga's questions.

'The pick-up. What cargo was your father picking up and where was he taking it?'

'I'm not sure where he was going. The truck company wouldn't tell me. They said it was confidential information. He was carrying light bulbs. That can't have been confidential.'

'Thank you,' said The Brain. 'You have been most clear and informative. I think it is obvious—to me at any rate—that our next stop must be the Furcht tunnel. We can do nothing tonight; the weather prevents it. If you can manage to wait until morning we'll enlist the help of the good Captain. You must stay here tonight. Is there anyone you need to call?'

'My aunt,' said Helga. 'I've been staying with her since my father ... well, since he disappeared.'

The Brain nodded.

'Sheldon, show Miss Poom to my room once she has called her aunt; I will be downstairs tonight doing some research.'

'You will hurry, won't you?' said Helga. 'I must find my father!'

'I am sure it will be fine, Miss Poom,' said The Brain. 'Please do not worry.'

Helga looked like she was about to say something else. Instead, she turned and followed Sheldon out of the room.

The Brain turned away as she left, and gazed out of the window at the silent, snow-covered streets. He tapped his pipe against his teeth and thought about the conversation he'd had with Helga Poom. He had formed a few ideas, some of which were extremely disturbing, if not downright incredible. There was always the chance he was wrong, of course. But it was unlikely.

He was The Brain after all.

No, if there was one thing about this case that he was already sure of it was that, unless they were very lucky, Helga Poom was unlikely to set eyes on her father again.

4

Urs Bupka, the Latvian trumpeter, sat sadly in his dressing room backstage at *Eurovisionara Dong Ding*. His arms rested on his thighs and his head hung low in a pose of total misery.

What a complete and total meltdown of a disaster. The King Kong of catastrophes. The Frankenstein of foul-ups.

From outside he could hear the roar of applause rippling around the Geneva Arena. Bupka's closest rival for the *Eurovisionara* title, the all-girl trio Hoppi Loppi Poppiloppila from Finland, had just nailed their speed-metal version of *Ghetto Heaven*. They were a cinch.

'I no understand!' Bupka growled for the umpteenth time.

His manager, Oleg Sternfugg, a small fat man smoking a small fat cigar, sat on the make-up counter, his legs dangling.

'You blewed it baby!' said Sternfugg. 'Or, rather, you didn't! What the hell where you zinking?'

'It not my fault. Stupid trumpet would not blow! You should get me good trumpet! Not stupid, not-blow, useless piece of junk trumpet from stupid Two Lat Shop!'

'There was nozzink wrong with trumpet, Urs! That is plenty good trumpet from best trumpet store in all of Riga! You maybe have bad moment? Stage fright?'

Urs Bupka stood up so quickly he knocked over his chair.

'Listen, Oleg,' he snarled, coming up close to the little manager. 'If trumpet so damn good, then you blow! If it from good music store in Riga then it should blow plenty good, yes?'

He thrust the trumpet into Oleg Sternfugg's pudgy hand, stalked off back to the corner of the dressing room and kicked the wastebasket. Urs picked up his trusty tin tray and smacked himself over the head. It didn't help.

Oleg Sternfugg shook his head sadly. Urs was a good client, one of the best he'd handled in a long career and it was sad to see him like this. The *Eurovisionara* had been his passport out of the ultra-competitive Riga tin-tray novelty-act circuit. Now it was all gone, just like that, thanks to that non-sense with a perfectly good trumpet. Stage fright, nothing more, nothing less.

'Urs, I—'

'Blow it!' yelled Urs Bupka. 'Blow damn stupid trumpet!'

Oleg shrugged.

'Whatever you say, Urs.'

He wiped the mouthpiece with a white handkerchief, put the trumpet to his lips, sucked in a breath and blew.

Parp.

A miserable squeak dribbled out.

'I must have blow wrong,' said Oleg. He puffed his cheeks and blew again.

Parp.

'Aha!' Urs Bupka danced around his manager. 'See? See? I told you was stupid trumpet, by gosh!'

Oleg looked at the trumpet carefully. He unscrewed

the mouthpiece and held it up to his eye. 'Get me light,' he said.

Urs rummaged round in a supply cupboard and found a torch.

'Here,' said Oleg, pointing at the small end of the instrument. 'Shine here.'

Urs directed the beam of light down the trumpet's gleaming innards.

Instead of a clear, machine-milled hole, the inside of the trumpet was almost completely blocked by something white. It left only the smallest of openings for the air to get through. Oleg pinched the end of the white stuff between his fingertips and pulled. A long coil of what looked like rubbery string came out of the trumpet.

'*Meekfunchdo!*' whispered Urs, which was a very bad curse-word in the part of Latvia he'd been brought up in. '*Muchdi meekfunchdo!*'

Someone, or something, had filled the Latvian's trumpet with spaghetti.

5

Early on Sunday morning, while Sheldon's mum got busy burning the toast, cremating the bacon, and making sure that every last trace of flavour had been completely removed from the eggs, The Brain brought Captain Schnurrbart up to speed about Helga's missing father, and persuaded him to let them do some investigating at the Furcht tunnel.

'I suppose I could pull one or two strings,' the Captain said. 'Might make it a bit easier for you.'

He picked up his mobile phone and snapped out a few quick instructions. He listened for a few moments then clicked the phone shut again. 'All arranged,' he said. 'An officer will come and take you there. I'm afraid I can't come along. I have some business at HQ to take care of.'

Captain Schnurrbart took a sip of coffee and immediately spat it into the sink.

'*Mein gott*, Mary!' he spluttered, looking at the contents of his cup. 'What is this stuff?'

Mary held up a jar of coffee.

'Just your regular coffee, Hans,' she said, a hurt expression on her face. 'No need to blow your stack, love!'

Captain Schnurrbart peered at the coffee jar.

'Take another look, Mary,' he said, turning the jar around. 'This is a jar of *gravy granules*!'

'Oops,' said Mary. She picked up the Captain's cup and

looked round. 'Waste not, want not, eh? Anyone fancy a spot of gravy with breakfast today? No? Oh well.'

Captain Schnurrbart sucked the edge of his moustache. He looked like he was about to say something. He stopped himself at the last moment and turned to Helga.

'I am sure your father will show up safe and sound somewhere, my dear,' he said kindly. 'And I'm equally sure that Theo and Sheldon will do their best to find him.'

'Yes,' said Sheldon's mum through a thick black cloud of smoke. 'That's exactly who I'd turn to if I was looking for a missing person: these two fruit loops. Mind you, I suppose they *did* get Seany off the hook, so maybe they aren't that bad.'

She slapped a plate of something that might have been breakfast in front of Helga.

'Get that inside you, love,' she said as she headed for the laundry. 'Put hair on your chest. Well, you know what I mean.'

'Thank you, Mrs McGlone-Schnurrbart,' said Helga, who appeared not to have noticed Sheldon's frantic signals to tell her not, *on any account*, to actually *eat* anything his mother put in front of her.

Helga picked up her fork, speared one of the sausages and *put it into her mouth*. Not only that, she seemed to enjoy it. To say that Sheldon was impressed would be putting it mildly. The girl was magnificent. Fearless.

As Helga munched on his mother's noxious bangers, Sheldon steeled himself for whatever adventure lay ahead. In the cold, grey light of a Swiss winter morning, it was time for action and he wasn't going to let Helga down.

It was time to start making himself look good in front of her.

Mary came back from the laundry holding up a big pair of grey thermal underpants.

'Sheldon, you be sure and wear these today. It'll be freezing out there.'

Sheldon groaned and put his head down on the kitchen table. One day he'd have to do something about his mother.

Seriously.

She was getting out of hand.

It took longer than anticipated to travel the twenty or so kilometres north to the Furcht. In Lucce the traffic had ground to a most un-Swiss jam, after what looked like a massive system failure. Traffic lights blinked randomly at every intersection, first calling cars forward, then stopping them again, until every road was thoroughly snarled. Drivers got out of their cars and expressed their anger at each other. (As it was Switzerland, this merely involved plenty of tutting and chin-scratching. There were one or two hotheads who resorted to eyebrow raising and looking quite cross, but they were few and far between.)

'Interesting,' said The Brain, studying the confusion through the car window. 'Unusual for Switzerland.'

'Oh yeah,' said Sheldon, shaking his head. 'Really very interesting.'

Honestly, sometimes he wished The Brain would concentrate on the important stuff. Like finding Helga's dad, for instance, instead of goofing off looking at stupid traffic jams.

'Like being in Italy,' growled their driver, Officer Knut.

He flicked a switch and turned on the sirens. A pathway opened up in front of the SSSU car and they cut through the Lucce traffic like a hot wire through cheese.

The Brain sucked furiously on his pipe: a sure sign to the experienced Brain-watcher that he was thinking Very Hard Indeed.

The traffic opened up once they left the town and hit the motorway. Knut gunned the car towards the Furcht tunnel and they were there inside two minutes. He pulled the SSSU car into the parking lot of a small administrative building huddled tight against the mountain. Snow whipped past as the four of them stepped out in the lee of the mountain, just metres from the gaping mouth of the northern end of the tunnel. Sheldon wished he'd put those dumb thermal underpants on. It was bitterly, ridiculously, laughably cold. Traffic roared past, making conversation difficult, if not impossible. Huge trucks from every corner of Europe, their sides coated with dirty snow and ice, screamed into the tunnel like prehistoric monsters searching for prey.

It was no place for pedestrians.

'Wait please,' said Knut. 'I need to clear access with the Roads Authority people.'

He strode across the dirty snow towards the office and went inside.

'We should come here more often!' yelled Sheldon. 'Bring a picnic, make a day of it!'

The Brain flashed Sheldon a look.

'You do know that sarcasm is the lowest form of wit, don't you, Sheldon?'

'No,' said Sheldon. 'Really? I had no idea! Is it?'

The Brain rolled his eyes and turned his attention to the looming mass of the mountain through which the Furcht was cut.

Helga looked at the tunnel entrance.

'Do you think he's still in there somewhere?' she asked The Brain.

The Brain didn't reply straight away. He appeared to be considering what he was about to say. Then he nodded.

'Yes,' he said firmly. 'We *will* find your father Miss Poom. You have my word.'

Sheldon looked at him. That wasn't like The Brain. For a moment he'd almost seemed human. What could have got into him? Then it hit him like a punch to the belly. There could only be one reason why The Brain was acting all warm and fuzzy around Helga ... he must be in love with her, too!

The low down, double-dealing snake!

'Is there something wrong with your eyes, Sheldon?' asked Helga. 'They've gone all sort of squinty.'

'Nothing wrong with my eyes,' said Sheldon, looking at The Brain. 'I can see everything *very* clearly indeed!'

The Brain did not appear to have noticed. His attention was on the office where Officer Knut was talking to a man dressed in the uniform of the Swiss Road Authority. After a minute or two, Knut emerged with plastic laminated passes on lanyards. He handed them out, and the trio them hung around their necks.

'Over there,' said Knut, pointing to a small door set into the mountain. 'We'll need torches. He says there are some lights inside but he's not sure which ones are working.'

As Helga pulled the door open, The Brain produced a torch from his backpack and checked it was working. Then the four stepped into a quieter, warmer, darker world and closed the door behind them. The howling wind and the roar of the traffic instantly dulled. Officer Knut flicked a switch on a light attached to his gun and a powerful beam cut through the murk. The Brain rummaged around in his backpack once more and produced what looked like some sort of GPS gizmo. He glanced at it for a second or two before turning on his heel and striding purposefully round the bend in the shaft. There was a pause before The Brain stuck his head back out.

'Well?' he barked, his voice echoing. 'Are you coming?'

Helga trotted after The Brain. Sheldon came close behind with Knut taking point, his gun held at port arms, eyes scanning for threats. Even if this was just a bit of glorified babysitting, it wouldn't do his career any good if he managed to lose two of the boss's kids. He gave the task his full concentration as the four were swallowed up by the Furcht tunnel.

Five minutes later, The Brain stopped at what appeared to be a crossroads at the intersection of five passageways cut through the rock. Sheldon ran into the back of him.

'Is it totally necessary to stick *quite* so close to me, Sheldon?' said The Brain. 'I almost dropped the torch.'

'Um ... just making sure none of us get lost. It *is* quite dark down here, Brain.'

Sheldon tried to control his breathing. He didn't want to appear cowardly—especially not in front of the divine Miss Poom—but he had to admit, the tonnes of rock above him did make him nervous. Tunnels weren't really his thing; he didn't like getting into elevators much, never mind scuffling along under the Alps.

'Where do we start?' said Helga, peering into the gloom. 'This place is gigantic!'

'That is correct, Miss Poom, but I think you'll find that it is even bigger than you might have thought.'

The Brain looked at his GPS unit and pointed the torch beam towards the central passageway. 'This way,' he said.

After a couple of minutes, with Officer Knut following watchfully at the rear, The Brain stopped at a flight of stairs.

'It's probably a good idea for us to get our bearings first,' he said, climbing the steps towards a thick steel door. 'Sheldon, if you'd be so kind, I may need a little help with this door. It has not been opened for some time.'

Sheldon trotted to the door, and he and The Brain pulled as hard as they could. The door wouldn't budge an inch.

'It's stuck fast,' panted Sheldon. 'We'll never get it open.'

Before Officer Knut could lend a hand, Helga stepped forward. Bracing her feet against the wall she took hold of the handle and pulled the door open easily. A blast of warmer stale air swept out.

'Er, thanks,' said Sheldon. 'Pretty impressive.'

Helga shrugged. 'Gym class at the Ladies College is pretty full on,' she said, flexing her bicep. 'But you boys probably loosened it, or—'

'Yes, yes, all very interesting, but we're wasting time,' interrupted The Brain. He pointed the torch through the opening. 'Now if I can just find a light—'

'Are you sure you know what you're doing?' whispered Sheldon. 'This place could be dangerous.'

As he spoke, The Brain's fingers found the switch and rank after rank of fluorescent lights blinked to life.

'What is this?' gasped Sheldon. 'It's incredible!'

The space they were standing in was the size of a cathedral, at least. The ceiling soared above them, seven storeys high. A jumbo jet could easily have sat on the floor, wings and all. A series of tables ran down the centre of the space, with various smaller spaces arranged along the outer walls. Inside the nearest of these, Sheldon saw a fully operational surgical operating theatre. Against one section of the wall were stacked row upon row of canvas sleeping cots. At the end of the room a massive four-bladed fan set into the wall turned slowly, pushing the air towards their four dwarfed figures.

'It's a bomb shelter,' said Helga. 'My father told me about it once. He said he'd visited when he was at school.'

'The largest bomb shelter in the world,' said The Brain, his voice echoing around the room.

'Bomb shelter?' said Sheldon. 'I thought this place was a tunnel?'

The Brain nodded.

'That is correct Sheldon, the Furcht *is* a tunnel. A very big one, although, to be accurate, it is in fact two tunnels, running parallel to each other through the mountain. But the Furcht is also, or was until very recently, a highly equipped nuclear bomb shelter. The room we're standing in is the central dividing chamber that sits between the two tunnels. Only one of the "tunnels" is in operation as a road tunnel. The other was designed to shelter the population of Lucce—or twenty thousand of them at any rate—in the event of a nuclear war.'

Sheldon couldn't decide what would be worse: to be caught on the surface in a thermo-nuclear global war, or to be stuck under a bazillion tonnes of Switzerland for however many years it took for the fallout to clear. Either way, it wasn't an appetising choice.

'It's so dusty!' said Helga sneezing.

Sheldon stepped uncertainly down a flight of concrete steps and stood on the main floor level. 'There's everything here! Look. Is that a prison?'

He pointed to an area of the shelter that had bars across a window set into a door.

'I believe so,' said The Brain. 'Sadly, even after a nuclear war, some people would still choose the path of the criminal.'

The Brain wandered a few paces into the main hall, glancing up at the huge arched ceiling supported by massive concrete pillars.

'We are lucky to see this place at all. It's due to be closed down soon and many of these spaces are to be sealed off.'

'In three weeks time,' said Knut, nodding. 'It's been in the papers.'

'The problem, as I see it,' continued The Brain, his eyes glinting behind his thick glasses, 'is that the Furcht tunnel is more like a labyrinth—that's a maze, Sheldon—and finding even something as large as a truck would prove difficult.'

'So what are we doing here?' said Helga. She was looking up at a faded diagram attached to the wall. It was part of the Furcht layout.

'I said "difficult", Miss Poom, not impossible.'

The Brain fished around inside his backpack and produced a small gun.

'This is a little device I put together last night.'

'It looks like a ray gun,' said Sheldon.

'It is, or was until yesterday. A toy ray gun, Sheldon, that's correct. I was using it as a component in the Cheesotron. However, last night I grafted something else into it: a high-powered thermal imaging sensor capable of penetrating solid rock. I think it may help us locate the missing Mr Poom.'

The Brain slid a roll of papers from his backpack and laid them out on a nearby table. Helga and Sheldon gathered round while Officer Knut made sure the area was 'secure'.

'The plans for the Furcht,' said The Brain, smoothing the edges of the sheet down as he spoke. 'I downloaded them.'

With a thin white finger, he traced their route.

'This is where we are now. As you can see, the working tunnel, the one used by the traffic, is running alongside this chamber in that direction.'

He pointed to the left.

'That is the route—towards Italy—that Miss Poom's father will have been travelling. Now, look closely at the map. Here.'

The Brain pointed to a section of the road that branched off about halfway through the Furcht tunnel. Sheldon and Helga bent over the map. Sheldon could smell Helga's hair. Pine and almonds. For a moment he thought he might faint. With some difficulty he concentrated on what The Brain was saying.

'This is the only point in the Furcht that a truck of that

size would be able to leave the main tunnel. It is an access road to some smaller service shafts and tunnels. It is also the nearest point to the LURV complex, which I find most interesting. I suggest we start our search there.'

He pointed at the huge fans at the end of the hall.

'We can use the air ducts to get there quickly.'

The Brain rolled up the plans and slipped them into his backpack. Not for the first time, Sheldon wondered if The Brain had somehow invented a backpack that was ever-expanding. He seemed to have just about everything in there.

'What about Officer Knut?' said Helga, looking around. 'Isn't he supposed to be here?'

The Brain looked up.

'Yes, very true, Miss Poom. It is most unlike an SSSU officer to wander off.' He peered into a tunnel that led off the main room at right angles.

'I think he may have gone down here. There's nowhere else really for him to have gone.'

The three of them moved towards the entrance.

'Officer Knut?' called The Brain. 'Knut? Can you hear me?'

There was no answer. Sheldon looked questioningly at The Brain. The Brain took out a torch and pointed it down the tunnel.

'I can hear something,' said Helga. 'Listen.'

Faint sounds echoed out of the darkness.

'I don't like this,' said Sheldon. 'I mean, I don't like Helga being, um, exposed to, erm, unnecessary dangers. We should go ... abandon the search.'

'Abandon the search?' said Helga, the blood rising in her cheeks. 'Absolutely not!'

'Oh, OK, then,' said Sheldon, feeling he'd lost some valuable brownie points.

As The Brain turned to say something, the torch beam caught the figure of Knut running towards them, an unusual expression on his face.

He looked scared.

SSSU officers don't get scared, thought Sheldon. They just *don't*. Wasn't it against regulations or something?

'Run!' shouted Knut. 'Get out of here!'

A blip of white light zipped out of the darkness and caught Knut full on the back. He opened his mouth to say something and then he ... disappeared.

In his place was a small blue chicken.

'What the ...?' gasped Sheldon as The Brain dragged him away from the tunnel. Sheldon caught a glimpse of the shooter running towards them.

There was something familiar about the way the man ran, but Sheldon couldn't put his finger on it.

The Brain pointed towards the air vents.

'There!' he snapped. 'Quick!'

Helga was already moving towards the end of the hall, a determined gleam in her eyes.

'Come on, Sheldon!' she said over her shoulder. 'What are you waiting for?'

Sheldon scrambled after them towards the air ducts. The blades of the circulation fan sliced through the air with a soft *whoosh*. From a distance they had looked slow, harmless. Close up, the blades looked lethal. Each one was ten metres long and swept past them like a giant axe. With typical Swiss precision, the edges were sharp, clean and well cared for, even after years underground.

'WE'RE NEVER GOING TO MAKE IT!' Sheldon had to shout to make himself heard over the rushing air.

'NONSENSE,' yelled The Brain. 'PIECE OF CAKE.'

They stood on a narrow concrete ledge, the massive steel blades whirling past mere centimetres away. Sheldon could feel himself being buffeted by the air.

'OK, GENIUS,' he shouted, glancing at The Brain. He pointed at the concrete shelf that lay on the other side of the blades. 'HOW DO WE GET OVER THERE?'

'IT IS QUITE SIMPLE, SHELDON. THE FAN BLADES ARE ROTATING AT SIX REVOLUTIONS PER MINUTE. THERE ARE FOUR EQUIDISTANT BLADES, WHICH MEANS WE HAVE A TWO-POINT-FIVE-SECOND GAP IN WHICH TO JUMP THROUGH!'

The Brain glanced at the blades as they came round.

'IT'S ALL A QUESTION OF TIMING, DEAR BOY.'

'TIMING? WHAT DO YOU MEAN TI—NEEEEEAR-RRRGH!'

Without warning, The Brain had placed his hand in the centre of Sheldon's back and shoved him hard in the direction of the fan. Sheldon flew through the air, the steel blades brushing past him for a terrifying micro-second before he landed safely on the other side.

'YOU SEE?' shouted The Brain. 'TIMING.'

With that, he and Helga jumped effortlessly between the blades and landed nimbly next to Sheldon. Through the rotating blades, Sheldon glimpsed their pursuer coming into the main hall. He wore military-style clothing with a cap that plunged his face into deep shadow.

To Sheldon's relief, he seemed not to have spotted them where they stood (or, in Sheldon's case, lay) in a pool of darkest shadow behind the blades. The man who'd turned Officer Knut into a blue chicken clearly felt that they could not have made it through the fan. He moved away towards the centre of the hall.

Helga watched him go and then held out her hand. Sheldon took it and struggled to his feet, a wave of determination sweeping through him. If Helga was there, he could cope with anything!

They turned a corner and the noise from the filtration fans became bearable again.

'I think we may have lost him,' said The Brain.

'What about Knut?' said Sheldon. 'What are we going to do about him?'

The Brain took his pipe from his pocket and placed it between his teeth.

'We need to forget about the unfortunate Officer Knut until we can find a way back to the surface. In the meantime, I suggest we continue with our mission.'

'Continue with the mission?' said Sheldon. 'What do you mean, "continue with the mission"? Knut's been turned into a chicken!'

The Brain regarded Sheldon calmly.

'What do you suggest we do? Return towards the attacker? It is logical to continue.'

Helga nodded in agreement. 'He's right, Sheldon. There

is nothing else we can do until we find another way out and report to Captain Schnurrbart.'

Sheldon looked from one to the other before stepping closer to The Brain.

'Do you think it's safe?' he whispered. 'I mean, *I'm* not worried, obviously, but I'm thinking about, you know, Helga.'

Helga turned to Sheldon. 'It's my father who's missing,' she said. 'You don't need to worry about me. Now let's get moving.'

She set off impatiently down the tunnel. The Brain looked at Sheldon and raised his eyebrows.

'Oh, shut up!' said Sheldon.

6

Every officer in the crack Swiss Scientific SWAT Unit has, as part of his essential equipment, a personalised state-of-the-art high-performance Shcheckler and Broon radio. These radios, not yet available on the open market, have many useful features, which include the ability to receive signals underwater, through steel, through rock and in deep forest regions of the world. They also have internet access, satellite-linked email facility and can hold a quite astonishing amount of information.

Last, but by no means least, they have the very useful ability, if destroyed, to issue an automatic last known position signal back to the SSSU headquarters.

A flashing red light on a computer screen gave the duty operator a lot of information. One click revealed the radio's precise geographical location, the time the signal was sent, and the name of the officer it belonged to.

'Captain,' said the duty operator, leaning forward to look at the screen. 'You might want to look at this.'

Captain Schnurrbart rubbed his moustache and crossed the room.

'Yes?'

'It's Knut,' said the operator. 'He's gone offline.'

'Call him on the back-up,' said Schnurrbart.

The operator tapped his keyboard and opened up the

personalised mobile phone that Knut, and all SSSU operatives, would have clipped to an inside pocket.

'Not a thing,' said the operator. 'It's just ringing.'

Schnurrbart straightened up. 'Keep trying. It might just
be a technical glitch.'

'There is something else, sir,' said the operator.

'Yes?'

'Officer Knut was the officer assigned to take your ...
sons to the Furcht Tunnel.'

Captain Schnurrbart didn't panic. Commanding officers
in the SSSU don't panic. Even the tea lady at the SSSU
headquarters has been trained to deal with emergencies in
a calm manner. Captain Schnurrbart's moustache simply
twitched a micro-millimetre to the left.

'Get me a car,' he growled, already walking purposefully
towards the HQ lift. 'And three active duty officers. I'm
going to the Furcht.'

On his way down to the underground garage, Schnurrbart
reflected on what he knew about the Furcht situation, and
the more he thought about it the less he liked it. To put it
mildly, it was not like Knut to let anyone down, let alone
three children. One of the SSSU's most experienced field
officers, Knut would never, unless it was a technical problem
(which, this being Switzerland, was simply laughable), fail to
respond to his mobile. Then with a jolt, Captain Schnurrbart
remembered the traffic chaos. Hadn't that been a technical
problem?

Something was wrong. Very wrong. The question was,
what, exactly?

*

Ahead of The Brain, Helga and Sheldon, the concrete walls of the emergency shaft gave way to raw rock as if the engineers had come this far and run out of concrete. To Sheldon, the rock gave the shaft the appearance of a cave; a spooky, bat-infested, vampire's lair buried beneath millions of tonnes of solid rock. If Frankenstein's monster had lurched out from behind a rock he wouldn't have been surprised.

'We've been walking for hours,' he said. 'I mean, this is really fantastic being down here and everything but, if it's not too much trouble, I wouldn't mind finding Helga's dad or, better still, GETTING BACK OUT BEFORE THAT SHOOTY DUDE CATCHES UP WITH US!'

The Brain looked at his GPS unit. The green LED display gave his face a ghoulish tinge, adding to the atmosphere of evil. 'Just a little further should bring us to the intersection with that secondary route I suggested Mr Poom may have taken,' he said.

He continued moving forward, sweeping the torch beam from side to side, stopping here and there to inspect a crack, or an unusual rock formation.

'Is it me,' said Helga, 'or is this tunnel getting narrower?'

The Brain turned to look at her. 'I think you're right,' he nodded. 'It does seem to be smaller.'

Twenty metres further on there was no doubt. The three had to crouch to move along and Sheldon's claustrophobia was creeping up at an alarming rate.

'The strange thing is,' said The Brain, 'on the plans this passageway is marked as being the same dimensions throughout its length. Most curious.'

He signalled for them to continue down the tunnel.

After another uncomfortable minute or two, they could go no further. The tunnel had become too small for them to stand. Hunched over, their backs pressed against the rock, the three looked at the solid walls and then at each other.

'How odd,' said The Brain.

'I don't understand,' said Sheldon. 'If this is an emergency carbon radioxide thingamajig tunnel, or whatever, then shouldn't it, like, have somewhere to go?'

'Maybe it's a rock fall, a landslide or something?' suggested Helga.

'That's not a good thought to be having down here, Helga,' said Sheldon.

The Brain shook his head. 'It's not a rock fall. The floor, the walls: they're smooth. There are no loose stones, rubble or any indication there's been a landslide or tunnel collapse. This *is* the access tunnel. If your father was down here, this is where he would be. If your father drove the truck down the service side road, as I strongly suspect he did, then we should be somewhere close by.'

He rummaged around his backpack, produced a small 'wand' attached to a sleek black case with a glowing green LED screen set into it, and attached it to his imaging sensor.

'This will let me "see" a little way ahead. Perhaps there's a small door, or an alternate route somewhere.'

The Brain pressed the switch and waved the wand ahead of him in a series of slow arcs. Sheldon could see a red line slowly moving across and back like a radar sweep. On the screen the rock showed up as pale, luminous green.

'If there's anything here it should show up as a darker

green area. The reader responds to density. Now, let's see what we can see ...'

The Brain walked forward, slowly scanning the wand backwards and forwards, up and down across the bare rock wall. For a few minutes there was total silence.

A sharp electronic chirp signalled a hit. Sheldon and Helga crowded round the screen and looked over The Brain's shoulder as he moved the wand back to the position the signal had come from. An object shimmered dark green as The Brain swept the device past a point in the wall.

Sheldon couldn't believe what he saw on the thermal imager. He rubbed his eyes and looked at Helga for confirmation. She remained still but her eyes widened.

The Brain fiddled with the buttons on the side of the thermal imager and the object sprang into ghostly focus. There, buried deep inside ten metres of solid granite, was the unmistakable outline of a thirty-eight tonne commercial truck.

7

The man who had shot Officer Knut bent forward and examined a series of marks in the dust. He raised his head and sniffed the air like a dog.

Or a wolf.

Tracking the three kids through the tunnel had been a challenge, but one that he was more than capable of. He'd wasted a little time in the main hall before picking up their tracks again and cursed when he realised they had slipped from his grasp. He hadn't thought they would have the cunning to take the route through the fans. He made a mental note not to underestimate them again.

With time to make up, he moved swiftly through the shelter and leaped through the circulation fan as if it wasn't here. Through tunnel after tunnel he picked up the signs: a fresh scuff mark in the dust here, a shred of white tissue paper there. Signals pointing him in one direction as clearly as roadside arrows.

After a few minutes, he slowed and then stopped. He could hear voices. Not far now. He unhooked his weapon, dimmed his torch and crept forward into the darkness.

Just around a bend in the tunnel, The Brain, Sheldon and Helga stared at the rock face.

'I don't get what you're saying, Brain,' said Sheldon.

'Me neither,' said Helga. 'The truck *must* have been caught in a rock fall.'

The Brain shook his large head.

'I don't think that is the case, Miss Poom. There are no indicators of loose rock, cracks or any sort of debris that would have been left after a rock fall big enough to enclose a vehicle of that size.'

He looked down at the thermal image once again and tapped it with his pipe.

'Impossible though it may seem, the truck is *embedded* in the rock, almost as if it was a fossil and the rock had formed around it. Look at the density reading.'

'But what you're saying is insane!' cried Sheldon. 'The truck can't have been there for millions of years. It's a truck! It can't be more than five or six years old!'

'Nevertheless, Sheldon,' said The Brain quietly, 'that is exactly what we are presented with. This will require some thought.'

'And what about my father?' said Helga. 'Is ... is he ... in there?'

Sheldon couldn't look at her. If her father was in the truck there was only one conclusion: he'd be encased in thousands of tonnes of solid rock, a permanent tomb. He shuddered. The idea of being closed up in solid rock was one of Sheldon's very worst nightmares. He cast his eyes over the rock above his head and, for a moment, thought he was going to faint. Only by digging his nails into the palm of his hand, and reflecting on what a complete spanner he'd look in front of the lovely Helga, did he prevent himself from running headlong out of the Furcht, screaming like a three-year-old. He breathed deeply and tried to get the floor to stop moving about under his feet.

'We cannot assume anything,' said The Brain in his briskest tone. 'Not until we have extracted the truck.' He patted Helga's shoulder. 'We must wait.'

Without warning, the tunnel suddenly lit up with a brilliant white light. It took a second or two for Sheldon to realise what was happening. The man who'd turned Knut into a blue chicken had found them. Worse—if such a thing were possible—he was trying to do the same to them. Sheldon contemplated life as a blue chicken and gave it up as too depressing. Being Sheldon McGlone was no piece of cake but he was pretty sure it beat life as an odd-coloured farm animal. He dropped to the floor and sucked dust. As he fell, he caught a glimpse of the military figure silhouetted against the flickering muzzle flashes.

Sheldon noted with some surprise that he had automatically followed at least some of the training taught at the Ecole. He had lain down head pointing at the source of the gunfire, minimising the target exactly as he had been shown by Miss Urtl in Battle Conditions 101. He was also analysing their position.

On the whole, he wished he hadn't bothered.

Their position wasn't, to put it mildly, promising. Behind them, a dwindling tunnel led to a dead end. Ahead of them a seasoned professional soldier waited with a mysterious weapon. It didn't look good. Surely, it was only a matter of time before the man advanced down the tunnel and finished them off. To Sheldon it was a SUBAR situation: Stuffed Up Beyond All Recognition.

Then a thought: Helga! Where was she?

Sheldon risked a look around. Helga was pressed against the opposite wall of the tunnel, trying to make herself as small as possible. Sheldon jerked involuntarily and cried out to her before The Brain pulled his head back down. Not a moment too soon: a blast of white light slammed into the rock just above them and a chunk of the wall turned into a wriggling mass of unidentifiable insects.

'Helga's a sitting duck,' hissed Sheldon. 'We've got to do something!'

The Brain nodded. Sheldon was right, but if they moved they'd be blipped in seconds. It was something of a miracle that Helga hadn't already been hit. She must be well concealed. Either way, it was only a matter of time ...

Sheldon looked imploringly at The Brain, willing him to think of something. Perhaps he could rewire the thermal imager into a makeshift explosive or a supersonic matter transporter, or a ray gun, or *anything* remotely useful. But Sheldon knew it would take too long, even for someone with The Brain's talents. He wasn't Superman.

Sheldon pressed into the dust, wishing he could just blend with the particles and atoms of the rock itself. With a sudden *whump* Helga landed squarely beside him, knocking all the wind from his lungs.

'Oops,' she hissed. 'Sorry about that.'

'Don't ... mention ... it,' wheezed Sheldon.

Then, suddenly, as quickly as it had started, the shooting stopped.

Without thinking, Sheldon reached across and took Helga's hand. It was cold, and he didn't know if he was doing it to comfort her or him, but whatever the reason, he liked it. Although, given a choice, he'd have preferred to have been able to live a little longer to enjoy the sensation. Right now that didn't look very likely.

He dropped his head, closed his eyes and hoped it wouldn't be painful.

Suddenly, he heard the sound of gunfire, shouts, and then silence once again.

Footsteps approached. Slowly, cautiously. The clang of military heels on rock. Sheldon clung to Helga's hand like a drowning man to a life raft. Amazingly, Helga stayed as cool as if she were waiting for a train.

'I'm afraid I have formulated no effective strategy to extricate us from this predicament,' said The Brain.

'I was hoping you wouldn't say that,' said Sheldon. 'Mainly because I didn't understand it.'

'Perhaps we can rush him?' said Helga. 'At least go down fighting. I know a bit of karate.'

'Rush him?' said Sheldon. 'Have you seen the size of that guy? He'd swat us like flies. That's, of course, if he doesn't shoot us before we get anywhere near him!'

'You have a better idea?'

She had a point.

'Miss Poom is right, it's our only chance,' said The Brain. 'Ready? On three. One ... two ...'

A voice cut through the acrid pall of gun smoke.

'Theo? Sheldon? Are you there? Miss Poom?'

Captain Schnurrbart!

Sheldon leaped to his feet. The hugely reassuring figure of Captain Schnurrbart stood in front of them, tensed for action, gun at his side. Behind him, three SSSU operatives crouched, weapons at the ready. Of their attacker there was no sign.

'A spot of bother I see?' said the Captain, raising an eyebrow.

'Yes,' said The Brain, brushing rock dust and debris off his jacket. 'A little. We were just about to deal with it ourselves when you arrived.'

'Apologies for the late arrival,' said Captain Schnurrbart. 'It took Officer Pathfinder a little longer to track you than we'd have liked.'

'Not that we're not grateful or anything,' said Sheldon, whose heart rate had slowed to a manageable two hundred beats per minute from the eleventy-trillion beats it had been hammering out seconds ago.

'Yes, thank you so much,' said Helga. 'Who was that shooting at us, and why?'

'That, my dear Miss Poom,' replied Captain Schnurrbart, 'is a very interesting question.'

'Two questions,' said Sheldon. 'That's actually two questions.'

Captain Schnurrbart's moustache twitched slightly. 'Of course, Sheldon,' he said. 'In answer to the first question; we're not sure. He vanished as soon as we arrived on the scene. We'd be a lot nearer to answering your second question if we could get our hands on him. Now, can someone please explain what's going on around here?'

'He shot Officer Knut,' blurted Sheldon. 'And he, he ... turned him into a chicken. Or at least we think it was a chicken. We didn't wait around long enough to check.'

The Brain was inspecting the tunnel walls near where the shooter had been. 'Curious,' he murmured.

'What is?' said Helga. She wandered over to inspect the rock face.

'There's no sign of a door,' said The Brain. 'Not a trace of any secret exit, nowhere for our pursuer to have gone to. And yet gone he most certainly has. It is most curious.'

Helga turned to Captain Schnurrbart. 'We found something in the rock. A truck. My father's truck we think. Show him. Theo.'

The Brain held out the thermal imager for the Captain.

Schnurrbart looked at the screen and then glanced at The Brain.

'Theo, is this what I think it is?'

The Brain nodded.

'It appears so, Captain. The truck is completely encased in rock. It's impossible, yet the evidence is in front of our eyes.'

'Any thoughts?' said Captain Schnurrbart.

'I'm thinking we need to bring in The Mole,' said The Brain.

Captain Schnurrbart nodded as if what The Brain had said made sense. 'Indeed,' he said.

'So what now?' asked Helga. 'What are we going to do?'

Captain Schnurrbart took out his radio and tapped at the keys. While waiting for a connection, he looked at Helga. 'We dig.'

8

Naturally, the SSSU being the SSSU, digging did not mean using anything as ordinary as shovels or picks. Instead, within an hour of the Captain's orders, the cramped tunnel was a hive of incredible scientific activity. Arc lights lit up the scene as boiler-suited SSSU operatives squeezed past each other in the confined space, bringing in various efficient-looking bits of machinery and electronics. The whole operation looked smooth and determined, if a little crowded. With an SSSU officer down, no-one was wasting any time.

'We'll get through to the truck before too long,' said the Captain to Helga.

He left unspoken the thought that everyone was having: once they did get through to the buried truck, what were they going to find inside?

A machine that looked like a large coiled spring mounted on a small bulldozer approached the rock face. The officer on board pulled down his protective visor as, with a hum, the coil began to glow.

'Everyone back,' ordered Captain Schnurrbart.

He didn't have to say anything else. The tunnel, already overcrowded and overheated, was getting more uncomfortable with each passing minute. Sheldon scooted back to a wider point and tried to get his claustrophobia back under control. If he'd been the worrying kind, he'd have sworn that the tunnel was continuing to get narrower. To take his mind off the idea of being smothered under the mountain, he asked The Brain about the drill.

'The Mole? It's a frequency modulation drill,' said The Brain.

Sheldon nodded as if frequency modulation was something he knew plenty about, when, in fact, everything he knew about frequency modulation drills could be written on the back of a particularly small stamp. 'I've heard about them, of course, but haven't actually seen one until now,' he said. 'Most interesting.'

The Mole worked by sending a series of electric pulse waves at the rock face. Everything in the universe, explained The Brain, has a certain tolerance to frequencies. If an opera singer hits a high note, he or she can shatter glass. The theory behind The Mole was that if you sent a signal pitched at the same frequency as another object, it should cause the object to dissolve into its component particles. Or something like that. Sheldon wasn't paying complete attention.

For one thing, Helga kept moving into his line of vision and, each time she did, Sheldon found his mind drifting. He thought about asking The Brain if Helga's hair reminded him of a field of gently waving, rain-sprinkled corn and her lips of sweet red rose petals kissed by the sun, but realised in the nick of time how much of an idiot he would sound. Besides, he didn't want to give The Brain any encouragement with Helga. What if he fancied her too? Where would Sheldon be then, eh?

To be honest, now that Sheldon thought about it, the idea that The Brain would make a move on Helga didn't seem particularly likely. He seemed to be more interested in The Mole. Sheldon simply couldn't imagine The Brain ever unbending enough to try anything with a girl.

It took about an hour for most of the rock surrounding the truck to be moved. The Mole had also widened the tunnel around the truck enabling SSSU operatives to move in.

'Miss Poom? Is this …?' said Captain Schnurrbart indicating the truck.

Helga nodded. 'I think so,' she said, her voice faltering. 'I mean, one truck looks very like another. But it could be his.'

'We're almost at the cab,' said Captain Schnurrbart. 'Let's go easy now.'

Helga's face was strained. Sheldon could feel his own face showing almost as much anxiety as hers. All he could think of was the day he'd been told about the sinking of *The Coreal* and his own father's death. It had been the very worst day of his life. Was the same thing about to happen to Helga? He could hardly bear it.

Captain Schnurrbart signalled to The Brain.

'Come, Miss Poom,' said The Brain. 'It may be best if we let the Captain and his team take things from here.' He led Helga away from the truck.

'No!' she snapped, with an impatient gesture, and walked back towards the truck. 'I need to see!'

Captain Schnurrbart sighed and signalled to the SSSU operatives standing by the cab door. 'Open it.'

Helga hurried forward. The door to the cab was stuck. Two large SSSU men braced themselves against the body of the vehicle and gave an almighty heave. The cab door flew open in a thick cloud of dust.

Coughing, Helga flapped the air in front of her until the dust slowly subsided.

The cab was empty.

Helga gasped and put her hand to her mouth. Sheldon let out a long breath and relaxed his jaw muscles. He realised he'd been grinding his teeth, fully expecting to see Helga's dead father.

'Thank God,' breathed Helga. Sheldon reached for her hand and squeezed it. 'I guess no news is sometimes good news, eh?' he said.

She nodded, her face white in the arc lights.

'You can stop squeezing now,' she said, glancing down at her hand. 'I think you're cutting off the blood supply.'

'Sorry,' said Sheldon.

Helga smiled and rubbed her fingers. 'That's OK,' she said and turned her attention back to the truck.

The cab was full of the usual signs of a scruffy truck driver: grubby maps, discarded soft drink cans, newspapers, empty Styrofoam burger-cartons, an almost empty, scrunched-up bag of chocolate raisins. The Brain inspected everything closely, but there was little of interest. Whoever had driven the truck into the service tunnel was long gone.

Sheldon idly picked up a raisin from the seat of the truck, popped it in his mouth and pocketed a few more. It seemed like an awfully long time since he'd eaten and you never knew when the next meal stop was going to be. As it was, the raisin was tasteless. Must have been there too long, thought Sheldon, even for me.

'What are you eating?' The Brain asked.

'Nn-mnnthin,' said Sheldon. He swallowed and followed the others to the rear of the truck, the other raisins jiggling guiltily in his pocket.

The fact that the truck was empty didn't prove anything, Sheldon supposed. On the one hand they hadn't (as Helga must have feared) found her father's body. On the other, they were still seemingly no nearer to finding him.

Captain Schnurrbart dropped down from the cab, went to the back of the truck, took hold of a heavy latch and swung open one of the doors to the container section. An SSSU officer did the same on the other side.

They all peered in. At first glance, the container appeared to be empty. Then, as the light from Captain Schnurrbart's torch swept over the interior, they noticed a small metal case about the size of a biscuit tin.

'I thought you said your father was picking up something from Lucce?' said Sheldon to Helga.

'He was.'

'Seems like an awfully big truck for a small load of light bulbs,' said Captain Schnurrbart. 'Hardly worth the effort, I'd have thought. Still, we can have a proper look at the whole thing back at the lab.'

The Brain was inspecting the tyres, which were squashed almost flat. He took out a small pen-like device and pressed one end into a tire valve.

'Pressure normal,' he said, taking out the pressure gauge and reading the result.

Helga looked down, puzzled.

'They look flat. How can the pressure be normal?'

'That,' said The Brain, 'is a very interesting question, Miss Poom. But I would predict that the Captain is going to have no end of trouble removing the truck back to HQ for inspection.'

'Can't they just drive it?' said Sheldon. 'What's the problem?'

Before The Brain could speak, the truck's engine roared into life. An SSSU officer sat in the driver's seat as other officers waited to guide him back out towards the intersection with the main autobahn tunnel.

Except the truck wouldn't move.

The driver floored the accelerator. The massive engine whined with the effort. The truck wheels turned fractionally before coming to a halt. 'The damn thing won't move, sir,' he yelled back to Captain Schnurrbart. 'Must be an engine problem.'

The Brain shook his head. 'I'm no expert, Captain, but that engine sounded in good shape to me. If I were to hazard a guess I would say that the truck is too heavy.'

'Too heavy?' said Sheldon. 'It's empty.'

'Nevertheless, look at the evidence. We have tyres inflated to normal pressure, yet squashed almost flat. We have an engine that is capable of pulling a fully loaded thirty-eight tonne truck. The truck is totally free of any surrounding rock. And yet the machine will not move. The only logical explanation is excess weight.'

Captain Schnurrbart stroked his moustache. The Brain wasn't often wrong. 'Let's take a closer look at that metal case,' he said.

The Brain put a hand on the Captain's arm. 'I'd take

more than a little care with that case, Captain. A lot of strange things have happened since that truck came inside the Furcht.'

'You're right, Theo. Let's get a Protection Zone established.'

Five minutes later the SSSU had rigged up a protective reinforced glass screen around the back of the truck and all personnel moved back behind it. Everyone watched from a remote station as Captain Schnurrbart, dressed from head to toe in thick protective clothing, walked awkwardly towards the truck. A small video camera in his visor relayed images back to the watching SSSU operatives.

'Receiving?' Captain Schnurrbart's voice crackled through the monitor.

'Affirmative, Captain. Images clear, readings steady. You're good to go.'

Close to the truck, Schnurrbart produced a Geiger counter that would detect even low levels of radiation. If the case proved to be full of plutonium, or some other dangerous material, they may all have been exposed already.

The Geiger counter clicked noisily as Schnurrbart moved further into the truck. Any rise in the frequency of the clicks would indicate the presence of dangerously high levels of radiation.

He held his breath as he passed the Geiger wand over the case.

Nothing.

Schnurrbart breathed steadily into his mask. 'Negative reading,' he said. 'I'm going to open the case.'

The Brain bent closer to the monitor as the Captain

took out a pair of heavy tongs and carefully lifted the lid of the case. Sheldon flinched involuntarily. The possibility that it was a bomb had occurred to him, as it had to everyone else.

'It's not a bomb, I am sure of it,' whispered The Brain. 'The Captain knows that, Sheldon.'

The case was open and Schnurrbart got a clear view.

It was completely empty.

9

Two hundred metres above Sheldon, and utterly unaware of the drama taking place beneath his feet, Otto Phleminger, a red-faced cow farmer, picked a large chunk of steak from one of his back teeth and stopped in the middle of a snow-covered meadow to get his breath back.

Otto had a problem.

The problem was Heloise, Otto's prize Polled Pinzgau cow, who had won the Gold Medal for Otto at the Shlammagammerau Farm Festival the last two years running and was an absolute stone-cold certainty for this year's medal. Heloise was a perfect Pinzgau, a princess of Pinzgaus. In addition to the Shlammagammerau glory, she had given Otto a lovely crop of fine young calves that had fetched high prices at the slaughterhouse. Heloise herself, once she got this year's medal in the bag and popped out another calf or two, would be turned into choice cuts herself, and Otto could hardly wait. If there was one thing he liked it was a nice, juicy red steak. As a matter of fact, the steak he'd been enjoying for lunch was from one of Heloise's offspring and very tasty it had been.

But now Heloise was in trouble.

Otto knew she was in trouble for two reasons. Firstly, she had got loose from her centrally heated pen again (this was the fourth or fifth time in as many weeks) and was now lost somewhere on the mountainside; secondly, because Heloise was making a lot of noise about it. Never a cow to suffer in silence, Heloise always let Otto know when something wasn't to her satisfaction; whether it was the wrong type of straw, or a slight delay in getting milked. Her distinctive moo—a kind of low, quavering, aristocratic moan of a moo—rolled out across the snow-covered meadow and plucked at Otto's heartstrings. He loved that cow—or, at least, loved the rewards that Heloise brought—and couldn't bear the idea of harm coming to her. Before, that is, her trip to the Shlammagammerau and the slaughterhouse. To complicate matters, Otto thought Heloise might have been expecting another calf. He didn't want to lose that little goldmine too.

'Heloise,' he yelled. 'Hold on Heloise my dear. Daddy's coming!'

Otto hurried as fast as his chubby legs could carry him in the direction of the sound. He floundered through the snow, slipping with the effort. It had been some time since Otto had done this type of chasing around after a cow. Normally he was less a hands-on type of farmer and more the kind who sits in a warm office and emails his staff to see to the details. But recently Otto had noticed that the normal smooth running of the farm had been plagued by distinctly un-Swiss problems. A few days ago one cow had produced blue milk. Only yesterday the automatic milking machine had tried to milk fifteen bullocks that had, somehow strayed into the milking parlour. It had taken three workers all day to calm the bullocks down. A sack of feed pellets had turned out to contain a mass of brightly coloured Amazonian tree frogs, a type of frog that did not exist in Switzerland and most certainly should not have been delivered in sacks of cow food. Otto had looked it up on the internet.

More worryingly, Heloise had been acting very strangely indeed. Her weight had gone up, something Otto was all in favour of, and then, just as quickly, gone back down again. It was a mystery, and Otto did not care for mysteries. He liked certainty, order, precision. And he definitely did not want to be traipsing around in the snow looking for a missing cow when he could have been back in his warm office drinking hot chocolate.

As far as Heloise was concerned, however, Otto only trusted one person to keep her happy and in full, medal-winning form. Himself.

At least the snowfall had stopped and the weak wintry sun was doing its best to put a brave face on the weather.

'Heloise,' Otto shouted again. 'Heloise!'

Heloise's answer came from close by, behind a rise over to Otto's left, near a low stand of trees. He turned in that direction and clambered up the snow bank.

'*Mooooooooooooo!*'

Otto crested the hill and scanned the trees, gasping for breath in the thin mountain air.

At first he couldn't see any sign of the cow. Then Otto's eye caught a sudden movement. A shadow, blue-white on the snow, was moving fast in his direction. Disoriented, Otto stumbled as a huge *thing* whirled out of the trees in a confusing blur of black and white.

Panicked, he flailed wildly.

'*Yaaaargh!*'

Otto looked around, his breath steaming in front of him. What was *that*?

Then there was movement again. He turned, but the sun was in his eyes and all he saw was a large shape silhouetted against the light. It was a bird. No, not a bird. It was too big. And yet there was something familiar about the shape that was now hurtling towards him. Otto turned and ran slipping and rolling back down the slope just as something caught him a glancing blow to the head. Otto cartwheeled through the air. As he did so he glimpsed curved talons, inky black, crow-like feathers and a pink, wobbling udder.

Heloise.

Otto lay on his back and looked at the sky. He rubbed his eyes in disbelief. Swooping in on outstretched wings, claws extended towards him, was Heloise. A new, not necessarily improved, Heloise.

With a moo that sounded like the screech of a pterodactyl hunting prey, Heloise latched her front claws onto Otto's shoulders and hoisted him clear of the ground. One of his gumboots fell off and landed in the snow. Otto shrieked and flapped wildly. It was no use; the cow's talons had him in their deadly grip. Heloise flew upwards, carrying Otto as easily as if he were a rag doll. Otto looked up and saw Heloise clearly for the first time. Her medal-winning body was unchanged, as were her pink udders and beautifully curled horns. But instead of hooves, she now sported a set of hawk-like claws, and from her shoulders a gigantic pair of black, eagle-like wings flapped effortlessly, pulling her upwards on a thermal current.

Otto gave a low groan, not too different from one of

Heloise's moos, and fainted. Heloise increased her speed. Up and up she flew towards the jagged mountain peaks, rags of cloud clinging to the white and grey forbidding faces.

In a few short minutes she'd reached her destination. She circled one of the most isolated outcrops and glided gently to a round nest built on the very peak. As Heloise approached, the noise level increased. Three mooing, squawking eagle-cow chicks opened their mouths and flapped their stubby little wings with excitement.

'*Moooooo!*' said Heloise and dropped Otto into the nest.

Dinner was served.

10

An empty truck that carried nothing, its driver missing. And now this.

Captain Schnurrbart looked at The Brain. 'What do you think, Theo?'

They had left the Protection Zone and were standing inside the truck looking at the case.

'I think,' said The Brain after a small pause, 'that it will be interesting to see if you can pick that case up.'

Captain Schnurrbart blinked. 'It is empty, Theo. Quite empty.'

'Then it should present little difficulty.'

The Captain snorted. In a quick motion he bent, grasped the metal handle of the case and lifted. It didn't budge a centimetre. He flashed a glance at The Brain and redoubled his efforts. The Captain's muscles bulged and his face grew red with the effort. The case didn't move. He relaxed and straightened up. 'It must be fixed to the floor,' he said.

The Brain shook his head. 'That is possible, but I think unlikely.'

'Then what is it?' said Sheldon. 'Why can't he lift it?'

The Brain jabbed his pipe into his mouth. 'Think, dear boy, think. When you have exhausted all other possibilities there will only be one explanation that remains.'

Sheldon looked none the wiser.

'Let us look at the evidence. Helga's father picks up a delivery from Lucce. He then goes missing and his truck turns up embedded in rock that is many millions of years old. The tyres on the truck are fully inflated yet they are compressed in the manner as they would be if carrying a heavy load. The truck was driven here, that much is obvious. Which leads to several conclusions. One conclusion is that the truck is getting heavier. Secondly, it is the contents of the case that is causing the truck to increase in weight. Thirdly, I also believe, although this is still a theory, that the case is responsible for the truck becoming embedded in the rock.'

'But it's empty,' said Helga. 'Look!'

'I must disagree, Miss Poom. I rather think the Captain now has an idea about what's in the case.'

Captain Schnurrbart stroked his moustache and nodded thoughtfully. 'Could it be?' he said softly to The Brain.

'It fits the facts, Captain.'

'What fits the facts?' said Helga. 'What are you talking about?'

'Yeah!' said Sheldon, 'what *are* you talking about?' His head was buzzing slightly.

Neither The Brain nor Captain Schnurrbart replied. The Brain produced his high-powered magnifying glass, and he and the Captain bent down to the case. 'Look.'

Through the lens, the Captain saw a tiny blue-black ball, a mere speck of material. If it wasn't for its spherical shape it would have looked like a grain of sand or a piece of discarded lint. Captain Schnurrbart leaned closer and, as he did so, the atmosphere inside the truck seemed to throb with electricity. The magnifying glass disappeared and in his hand the Captain held a bunch of odd-looking red flowers. The flowers opened their petals and began to sing. It was a high-pitched, thin sound, but quite definitely singing.

'*La, la, de, la-la, laaaa . . .*' trilled the flowers.

'What the—' said the Captain, dropping them like they were radioactive.

'*La, la, la, laa-laaaa, dum-ti-dum, doo . . .*' sang the flowers from the floor of the truck.

'Hey,' said Sheldon. 'They're not too bad!'

The Brain looked at the flowers. 'I suggest we move to a safe distance again until we can get this substance sealed,' he said. 'Before anything else happens.' He looked at the Captain. 'Are you thinking what I'm thinking?'

Captain Schnurrbart nodded. 'Professor Duzzent,' he said in a strange voice. The blood had drained from his face. 'Quick everyone, get back to the Protection Zone!'

He sprang upright and pulled everyone out of the truck.

'*La, la, la-laa-laaaa, dum-ti-doo, dee, dum, dum, doo-dooo . . .*' sang the flowers.

'I don't understand,' said Helga once they were all back behind the protective glass and away from the singing flowers. 'Who is Professor Duzzent? And what happened to that magnifying glass?'

'That's a very good question, Miss Poom,' said The Brain. 'If I'm right, and as you know I usually am, then the substance inside that case is something very worrying indeed. Physicists have talked about the existence of dark matter for years but have had little success in observing it. Six years ago, a brilliant but unstable scientist called Professor Dirk Duzzent claimed he had found a completely new substance that caused—under certain conditions, a power surge for example—anything coming in contact with it to change places, randomly, with something from another universe.'

'What happened to Duzzent?' said Sheldon.

'He disappeared. In the morning there was no sign of him although his lab contained a very confused, one-metre tall man wearing clothes made from a plastic-like substance unknown on this planet. He spoke no known language and was, eventually, admitted to a mental institution where he remains to this day. The SSSU have suspected the existence of another type of dark matter for some time. After this event the substance was named after Professor Duzzent. Duzzent Matter.'

'Why doesn't it matter?' said Sheldon, confused.

'No,' said The Brain. 'It's *called* Duzzent Matter, after Professor Duzzent, see?'

'Yes, but what *is* it?' said Helga. 'And what does it have to do with my father's disappearance?'

'Well, for one thing, dark matter is very, very heavy. Which is why the truck won't move. Dark matter, we think, also pulls other atoms towards it, like a tiny, but very powerful, vacuum cleaner, which is perhaps why the truck got stuck. But *Duzzent* Matter does everything dark matter does, except it is much more ...'

The Brain took off his glasses and rubbed them with a handkerchief. He replaced them and looked at Captain Schnurrbart, who shrugged.

'Yes?' said Sheldon impatiently. 'Much more what?'

'Silly,' said The Brain. 'Duzzent Matter is the silliest substance in the universe.'

'Silly?' said Sheldon.

'What do you mean "silly"?' said Helga. 'And why would being *silly* be a problem? How does a little speck of stuff get "silly"?'

'The whole thing sounds stupid if you ask me!' said Sheldon.

'Not "stupid" old bean,' said The Brain. '"Silly". There's a world of difference.'

Sometimes The Brain could be very annoying, thought Sheldon. This was one of those times.

'Have you ever heard of the Bermuda Triangle?' said The Brain. 'The Figlock Baby? Roswell?'

Sheldon shook his head. Even Helga looked blank.

'What are they?' asked Sheldon. 'Rock bands?'

'No,' said The Brain. 'They are all, I believe, instances of Duzzent Matter "breaking in" to our world. The Bermuda Triangle is an area near Bermuda which, from time to time, appears to "swallow" planes and ships. They disappear without trace and no wreckage is ever found. Our idea is that that may be Duzzent Matter at work and the planes are being "replaced" by things, creatures from other universes. If they happen to be things that can't fly or float, then we would never find a trace of them, would we? It may also be that Duzzent Matter sometimes opens up gateways to alternate universes rather than "replacing" objects or people.'

'Difficult to prove,' said Sheldon.

'Absolutely,' agreed The Brain. 'But the world is littered with unexplained phenomena like this. Silly, strange, disturb-ing events. "Alien" landings. UFOs. American presidents.

Did you know that more than ten million people "disappear" every year? Not all of them are runaways. One of the SSSU researchers has a theory that more than seventy percent of Hollywood actors are products of Duzzent Matter. What about darts players? Train spotters? People who get into the Guinness Book of Records? There's a man in there who eats planes! Surely there's a question mark over him being human? And don't tell me you haven't ever seen someone and thought "he's from another planet"? What about wig manufacturers? Who do you think *buys* all those wigs? Creatures, people from other universes trying to blend in, that's who! And there's a lot of evidence that entire *cities* are the product of Duzzent Matter. How else can you explain Las Vegas?'

'OK, OK, I get the picture: weird stuff happens and you think this Duzzent Matter is the cause.'

'Precisely, old top,' said The Brain. 'Now, I suggest that it could also be dangerous to remain here.'

Captain Schnurrbart nodded. 'I am in agreement. This phenomenon is something that will have to be investigated fully in the safety of a controlled laboratory.'

He turned to an SSSU officer.

'Bag it and tag it, Mueller. Get the hydraulic power lifter in: that gizmo would shift anything. Let's get this thing back to HQ and run it through the grinder. I want full micro-atomic gamma obs, spectrometer analysis, goober mechanics check, the complete works on this little mess, got it? And take no chances. If you get so much as a sniff of any power surge you get clear. I don't want to find you've been replaced by a bunch of flowers.'

Mueller snapped off a smart salute and the SSSU sprang into fevered activity.

'What about us?' said Sheldon. 'What do we do now?'

'Tea, I think,' said The Brain.

11

Two hours later Sheldon was cramming a creamy éclair into his mouth and feeling a lot better. He hadn't realised quite how horrible it had been in the Furcht tunnel. Now, safely back home, even the revolting smell of his mother's lasagne couldn't spoil his mood. And hungry! He'd forgotten how hungry he'd been. Just one measly dried-up raisin since breakfast. He slurped down another éclair (thankfully shop-bought) and began to pay attention to the conversation.

'Anyone else like some lasagne?' Sheldon's mum held up a plate on which sat what looked like the leftover from an alien autopsy.

'Oh, looks delish! But not for me mum!' Sheldon said, rubbing his stomach. 'I'm stuffed!'

Helga impressed Sheldon once more by taking the plate. There were only two possible explanations. Either Helga liked his mother's food (which was, of course, impossible) or, more likely, the manners she'd developed at the Alpine Ladies College etiquette classes kicked in when offered food. Either way, it was heroic.

Captain Schnurrbart also showed his heroic side, and the reason he'd been awarded three separate Legion de Valour medals, by reaching over and taking the plate of glop with every appearance of pleasure.

'I'll have some of that, Mary,' he said, with what looked

like a genuine smile. He lifted a forkful of lasagne to his mouth and took a large bite. 'Mmmm. Delicious!'

Mary McGlone-Schnurrbart beamed and bustled into the kitchen.

Sheldon had to give it to the Captain. The guy knew how to make sacrifices. 'So, what's the plan?' he said, licking a last blob of cream from his fingers.

'I think we know where our next stop is, don't you Captain?' said The Brain.

Schnurrbart stroked his moustache.

'Yes, I think you're right, Theo,' he said through a mouthful of charcoal. 'The trail clearly points to LURV.'

'So why don't we just head over there and wave some official papers round and find out what's happening?' said Helga. 'My father might be in there.'

'If only it was so simple, my dear,' said the Captain. 'We have very little hard evidence, and the people behind LURV are, on the face of it, part of the same team as us. Some of the world's greatest scientific minds are in LURV and they are not without a certain amount of power and influence. They wouldn't take kindly to us stomping across their territory. The machinery over there works extremely slowly and they wouldn't respond to threats. As the song says, you can't hurry LURV.'

'Besides,' said The Brain, 'I am of the opinion that whatever is happening at LURV may be happening *without* the full knowledge of those in charge. There are thousands upon thousands of experiments taking place there by scientists from many different countries, with many different governments involved—some of them not so choosy about cutting corners and taking risks. It is highly likely that what happened at the Furcht was *not* sanctioned by LURV, at least not officially. What we need is to get in there under-cover and take a look around. The tricky part will be getting into LURV without arousing suspicion.'

The Brain rubbed his chin while Captain Schnurrbart tapped his shiny boots against the wooden floor and did his best to swallow some more of his wife's lasagne. Inserting an undercover agent inside a suspicious environment was always a tricky procedure. Finding a way into one of the most pro-tected scientific research stations in Europe was not going to be an easy task, even for an organisation with the pull of the SSSU. This was going to take some thought.

Helga had been tapping away at a laptop on the kitchen counter. The LURV website was onscreen in front of her.

'It's quite simple to get in,' she said. 'We just book a school trip. They run tours every weekday.'

Sheldon smiled. It wasn't often you saw The Brain *and* the Captain lost for words. He winked at Helga, who smiled back at him.

'I like it,' said the Captain. 'Theo, please get this started will you? I'll make sure the school goes first thing Monday morning.' He picked a large piece of something rubbery from between his teeth and grimaced. 'Now if you will excuse me, I have, um, urgent business to attend to upstairs.'

He hurried from the room, a greenish tinge to his face.

'There must be *something* we can do before tomorrow,' said Helga.

Sheldon thought she must have a stronger digestive

system than the Captain's. Either that, or the Ladies College simply did not *permit* illness.

The Brain looked around. Mrs McGlone-Schnurrbart was in the kitchen looking distrustfully at a cookbook as if suspecting it might explode at any moment. Captain Schnurrbart had once mentioned he had a fondness for fondue and Mary wanted to surprise him. Sheldon wanted to be there when she served it: if he knew anything about his mother's cooking, she may well have discovered a new form of everlasting rubber.

Sure that he wasn't going to be overheard, The Brain unfolded a map on the dining table. 'There *is* something we can do, Miss Poom,' he whispered. 'That is, if you feel up to a little more adventure?'

'Of course,' said Helga. 'Anything.'

'This is a map of the region immediately around the LURV centre,' The Brain continued. 'As you can see, access is not easy. A single road services everything into the main control gates. Of course, once inside, the entire place becomes an underground city. What can be seen from the surface is merely the tip of a very large iceberg.'

'What *is* it about the Swiss and drilling into mountains?' said Sheldon. 'Everywhere you look they've got underground bunkers, tunnels, research stations ... Even the cheese is full of holes!'

'Or not,' said The Brain, looking meaningfully at Sheldon.

'I'm not going down any more holes,' said Sheldon firmly.

'No holes this time, old bean,' said The Brain. 'At least, I don't think so.'

'I don't care. I'm staying put tonight. I'm not going any-where near that LURV place, or any rock-sucking Dizzy Matter—'

'Duzzent Matter,' murmured The Brain.

'Whatever. I don't care what that silly stuff is called, I'm not going anywhere near it!'

There was a short silence.

Helga stood up. 'Then I'll go on my own,' she said, looking at Sheldon with her big green eyes. 'It is *my* father who's missing. Perhaps if you'd been through something like this you'd know how I feel and *do* something instead of sitting here.'

Sheldon and The Brain exchanged glances. Neither said anything. They didn't have to. Both knew only too well what it was like to lose a father—or even, in The Brain's case, a father *and* mother. But Helga didn't know that. Her lip trem-bled and her beautiful eyes—looking very like twin lagoons of emerald perfection, Sheldon couldn't help noticing—moistened. Sheldon knew if she so much as shed a single tear he'd single-handedly take on a battalion of under-ground psychos.

A fat tear slid silently from one of Helga's eyes and Sheldon was lost.

'What are you waiting for, Theo?' Sheldon barked. 'Let's get crying—I mean, let's get moving! It's time I dealt with my tears—I mean fears!'

After a pointed look at Sheldon, The Brain raised his left eyebrow two millimetres before tracing a finger along a dotted line that ran across a section of the map. He made a sound that might have been a cough before speaking. 'This is, I believe, a flaw in the LURV security,' he said. 'It's a secondary service road that runs to the rubbish collection depot. It can be reached by getting to this point—' he jabbed a finger at the map '—and scaling a small fence. I propose that we use tonight to gather what information we can from the LURV site. The more information we possess, the more fruitful will be our trip on Tuesday. What do you say?'

Sheldon slapped the table and looked at Helga. She was dabbing at her eyes with a white handkerchief. 'Let's do it,' he said.

12

'It's always at night, isn't it?'

The Brain looked at Sheldon. 'What is always at night, old top?'

'Sneaking round spooky places.' Sheldon gestured at their surroundings. 'In the movies, everyone always seems to sneak round these kinds of places at night. And now we're doing it.' He glanced hastily at Helga. 'Not that I'm not happy to be here,' he added lamely.

The snow squeaked beneath their feet as they walked, the black teeth of the Alps looming inkily against the black-blue sky. Sheldon felt, as he often did on the mountains, as if he were in a library or a church. He still hadn't become used to the odd light on the snow at night. Although it was obviously night-time, what light there was from the moon and the stars reflected off the snow and bathed everything in a soft, blue-tinged glow. It had snowed during the day and the trees looked as though they'd been iced by a baker with a heavy finger.

If they hadn't been on a dangerous mission, Sheldon might have even enjoyed the trip. His breath rose in a soft cloud as he tried to get the thin air into his lungs. Walking anywhere in the mountains was always tough and, despite the cold, Sheldon was hot. A thin trickle of sweat ran down his back and cooled unpleasantly at the base of his spine.

After sneaking out of the house at Schnarchen, it had taken them well over an hour to hike uphill from the train station at Lucce to the service road that fed into the LURV complex. Twice, headlights alerted them to approaching vehicles and they scurried clumsily into the snow-laden trees. It was hard going and, as they continued to climb, conversation ebbed away. Eventually they reached a point above LURV and The Brain stopped. From this position the road curved round and then up and over a section of the mountain, before sloping back down to LURV. By road it would take them another hour, at least, to reach the complex. After careful study of the map, and through the magic of Google Earth, The Brain had spotted a shortcut.

He unhooked his snowboard and placed it at his feet.

'I suggest we use our boards for the rest of the journey,' he said. 'It will save us considerable time and the moon is almost as good as daylight. Visibility shouldn't be a problem if we are careful.'

'No argument from me,' said Sheldon. It was already past midnight and he had to admit he was fading. The snowboard was just what he needed.

Helga, like almost every Swiss person, seemed to have been born wearing skis or a snowboard. She slid effortlessly between the black trees, carving out a smooth line for the others to follow. The Brain, surprisingly, was almost as good. He didn't have the natural grace of Helga, but his movements were precise and skilled. In fact, The Brain had never before been on a snowboard. He had picked up a book called *Teach Yourself Snowboarding* earlier in the day and, after a brief read, was confident he understood the theory.

When he had first tried snowboarding, Sheldon had looked like he'd strapped a plank of wood to his feet and fallen off a cliff. Nonetheless, after six mostly wintry months in Switzerland he was competent enough to keep up—just.

'Wait up, fellers,' he hissed, looking suspiciously at the forest that lay between them and the LURV complex. With a wobble that almost saw him flat on his back, he pushed off down the slope, following the tracks made by the others.

Once his heart had stopped doing the cha-cha, he began to enjoy himself. As he flew between the dark trees, Sheldon had to admit that snowboarding at midnight wasn't a bad way to pass the time, even if they were hurtling towards a secretive scientific research station that may or may not have been linked with the disappearance of Helga's father.

After a couple of minutes, they came to a halt at a wire fence that surrounded the LURV complex. Or, to be completely accurate, The Brain and Helga came to a halt. Sheldon only stopped when he smashed straight into the fence.

'Ow!' he groaned, pulling himself groggily to a sitting position.

'Very classy, Sheldon,' said The Brain. 'That helps keep all this hush-hush.'

'Are you OK?' asked Helga.

Sheldon nodded. 'I'll live,' he said.

The Brain motioned for them to move behind a rise that masked them from the LURV complex that lay below them, bathed in eerie orange light. 'Should be a tad more private here, I suggest,' he said, producing a pair of high-powered night-vision binoculars from his backpack. In fact, he had little need of them, such was the effect of the moonlight on the snow.

Sheldon rubbed his elbow and pointed at a cylindrical object about fifty metres away. 'What's that thing?' he asked.

'Looks like some sort of hatchway,' said The Brain. 'A bunker or something. What do you think?'

He passed the binoculars to Helga.

'It could be a ventilation shaft from the Furcht tunnel,' she said. 'We're right above it, you know. Remember the ventilation fans we had to jump through? The filtered air has to come out somewhere.'

'I think you might be right,' said The Brain.

Helga passed the binoculars to The Brain. Sheldon winked at her and she smiled.

'What do we do now?' said Sheldon.

'We wait,' said The Brain.

Somewhere in the distance a cow mooed.

A few minutes passed.

'Did you hear that?' asked Sheldon.

'What, the cow?' said Helga.

'No, after that. I could have sworn I heard someone yelling for help from way up there. Very faint.'

The three cocked their ears to the sky and listened.

'Oh, well,' said Sheldon. 'My mistake.'

The Brain turned his attention back to LURV. Everything seemed perfectly normal. Nothing you wouldn't have expected . . .

'Look!' said Helga, jogging The Brain's elbow. 'Something's moving out there!'

She was right.

The snow on top of the shaft lifted and a hatchway was flung back. Something big was climbing out of it. Cautiously, slowly, a strange dark shape emerged.

'What on earth is that?' whispered Sheldon.

Next to him, The Brain adjusted the night-vision function on the binoculars. 'By Jove!' he muttered softly.

'*Muffk pag shimcock*!' The thing grunted, shuffling into a position where the moonlight fell on it.

Helga gasped.

Sheldon rubbed his eyes.

It was a cuckoo clock.

An enormous, walking, shuffling, grunting, drooling, growling, cuckoo clock with a pointed, red-tiled roof, below which was a clearly recognisable clock face complete with numbers and ornate hands. Almost two o'clock. A window in the creature's forehead opened and a bright green cuckoo poked its head out and sounded the time. Sheldon rubbed his eyes in disbelief, his brain refusing to compute the information.

This simply could not be happening. Except that it was.

Next to him, The Brain came as close as he ever came to showing shock. He raised an eyebrow.

'*Ferknif*!' grunted the clock thing. '*Mishpit*!'

The cuckoo-clock creature had two thick, scaly legs glistening with a slime that left a slick on the snow as it walked. Beneath the clock face was what Sheldon presumed was its mouth; a gaping cavern filled with row upon row of sharp yellowish teeth that gnashed and clashed in a way that reminded Sheldon of one of those movie monsters that always seem to be roaming round abandoned spaceships on strange planets. The creature snorted and flicked its tail from side to side. The tail resembled the dangling weights usually found underneath cuckoo clocks. It didn't seem to have eyes, relying instead on three thin, flexible antennae that emerged from near its mouth.

It shambled around the storage area grunting hungrily in a way that turned Sheldon's bowels to water. The creature smacked its lips, dribbling large fat gobs of drool onto the snow. Sheldon had the horrible understanding that it was looking for something to eat.

Next to Sheldon, Helga stiffened. 'Looks hungry,' she said softly. 'I hope it's a vegetarian.'

A rabbit lolloped past, saw the clock and stopped. After the briefest pause, the rabbit took off across the snow. A slimy tentacle flashed through the air, caught the rabbit by the hind legs and dragged it straight into the clock's gaping mouth. With a wet crunch, the clock ate the rabbit in one bite.

'I guess that answers that question,' said Sheldon.

Two more things occurred to Sheldon at about the same time. Firstly, given the fact that they were halfway up a snow-covered alp completely free of takeaway joints, Sheldon guessed they were probably the tastiest items for miles around. Secondly, and very, *very* importantly, he had an overwhelming desire to not get eaten. Apart from anything else, being eaten by a mutant cuckoo clock was a completely ridiculous way to die.

From the hatchway, another cuckoo clock now emerged. Much smaller than the first. As they watched, a plastic-looking bird popped out of its head and sounded three high-pitched chirps before the clock dropped down onto the snow. It fell onto its back in the snow and wriggled furiously. The larger cuckoo clock ambled back towards the smaller clock and, using a slimy tentacle, raised it to its feet and pushed it in the direction of the trees.

'*Querk!*' said the large clock impatiently. '*Slurp quark buffkit!*'

A third creature, then a fourth and fifth, emerged from the hatch, chirruping as they rolled (like puppies, thought Sheldon) towards their mother. Or was it their father? The clocks began rummaging around in the bushes.

Behind them, another shape came up silently from the ventilation shaft.

'It's him!' hissed Sheldon. 'The guy who was shooting at us!'

'Sheldon, I do believe you're right!' said The Brain. 'Keep down.'

Sheldon didn't have to be told twice. Even though the new arrival wore a balaclava over his face there was no mistaking that build, that posture. He looked even more menacing than when they'd seen him in the Furcht.

'*Mufflcockspli shnapbanker! Merk!*' the big clock swore as it caught sight of the man. '*MOOSHPI! MOOSHPI!*' it shouted.

The smaller clocks scattered. The man in the balaclava cursed and lifted his weapon as he tried to get a sight on them.

The creature bellowed and its weighted tail lashed out, catching the shooter a vicious glancing blow that sent him sprawling in the snow. The delay allowed the small clocks to make it to the safety of a clump of trees.

The large cuckoo clock made a break for it, straight towards the rise where Sheldon, Helga and The Brain were hiding. Behind it, the man dropped to one knee and took careful aim.

A blip of white light zipped through the air and the clock fell forward without a sound. It was immediately replaced by a small glowing pyramid.

Satisfied, the shooter shouldered his weapon and pulled off his balaclava. He shook snow from his hair and, for the first time, the three observers saw his face clearly.

The Brain gave an involuntary twitch and Sheldon felt like he'd been hit with a taser. It was more unbelievable than seeing the mutant clock. The world turned upside down.

Standing before them, absent-mindedly brushing snow off his moustache, was none other than Captain Hans Schnurrbart of the Swiss Scientific SWAT Unit.

13

Captain Schnurrbart was dreaming.

Ordinarily, he did not dream. Dreaming, felt the Captain, was something of a waste of time and, on the whole, should be avoided by all sensible Swiss people. However, the Captain was only human and sometimes he simply could not avoid them.

In his dream, something was moving on his face, but he was helpless to do anything about it. Captain Schnurrbart had never told anybody, but he had a fear of spiders. And now a great big, hairy one was crawling over him! He wriggled furiously before realising the thing on his face wasn't a spider: it was his moustache. And it was alive.

The phone rang. Captain Schnurrbart snapped awake. He picked up the slim black phone and flipped it open, unconsciously checking his moustache for signs of life.

Beside him, Mrs McGlone-Schnurrbart turned over and pulled the covers over her head with a groan.

'Schnurrbart,' said Captain Schnurrbart in a low growl.

'Sorry to wake you, Captain,' said the voice on the other end of the line. 'Duty Officer Hefferning here, sir.'

'What is it, Hefferning?' Captain Schnurrbart twisted round to check the time. 'It's almost three. This better be good. And what on earth are those noises?'

'Yes, sir, sorry about that, sir. It's just that, well ... I think you ought to come down to HQ sir. We're getting some very um, strange . . . events happening.'

'Events? What do you mean "events"?'

Officer Hefferning hesitated. 'Well sir, it's hard to expl—'

Captain Schnurrbart interrupted.

'For goodness sake, Hefferning! I'll be down there directly. And if this turns out to be a wild goose chase, then heaven help you!'

Exactly twenty-one minutes later, Captain Schnurrbart strode into the SSSU HQ wearing a freshly pressed uniform and a scowl that would strip paint at ten paces. He was not in the mood for nonsense.

He pushed open the double doors to the main control room and looked around.

It was empty.

Captain Schnurrbart was not amused. It was an absolute rule that the main SSSU control room was to be staffed at all times. He went to the intercom microphone and snapped it on.

'Hefferning!' he barked. 'What in blazes are you up to, man? Where is everybody?'

There was a click of static and Hefferning's voice came through the intercom system, accompanied by a blizzard of background noise.

'Sorry, sir. I'm down in the lab. The large one, sir. You'll have to come down. They're everywhere!'

There was a click and Hefferning was gone.

Captain Schnurrbart was already out of the room, his

right hand flicking open the holster on his gun as he ran. He ignored the lift and took the stairs four at a time, his boots ringing on the bare concrete. Three floors down and he sprinted round the corner to the main laboratory. Coming from inside he could hear screams, the sound of objects being thrown and an unearthly honking sound. It sounded like a massacre. He moved forward quickly, his gun held steadily in front of him and kicked open the lab door.

As it swung open, a large green-and-gold-striped goose flew out, hotly pursued by Officer Hefferning. Hefferning saluted Captain Schnurrbart as he passed and threw himself at the goose. The goose honked madly and bit Hefferning hard on the upper arm. The two of them disappeared round the corner.

'Sorry, sir,' shouted Hefferning. 'Just let me get this goose under control.'

Captain Schnurrbart shook his head, stepped inside the lab and looked around.

The laboratory, one of the most highly developed and equipped anywhere in the world, was usually an oasis of calm, the only sounds those produced by the investigative experiments and tests taking place.

Now it was full of geese.

Noisy, honking, multi-coloured geese of a bewildering variety of sizes and shapes. They were being chased by the rest of the SSSU duty staff. Officer Schmidt had a blue goose the size of a small hippo in what looked like a Taiwanese death grip, but it seemed to be having little effect. The goose pecked at him angrily, its monstrous beak millimetres from his face. In another corner three bright pink geese, smaller than the blue one, but just as mean-looking, appeared to have Officer DeKooning trapped between a large centrifuge and a spectron analyser. He was holding the geese at bay with a baton that he swung in their faces. To Captain Schnurrbart's left, a flock of geese was cir-cling the truck they'd brought in from the Furcht tunnel. Officers Vermorel, Pathfinder and Frimmel stood helplessly on the trucks exposed floor, marooned by the seemingly endless sea of birds honking below them.

It was chaos.

It was silly.

It was time to get this under control.

Captain Schnurrbart was not a violent man. But when the need arose he didn't hesitate. He scanned the room until he found what he was looking for. The biggest, most vicious-looking goose in the room; a huge bruiser of a bird, black-blue in colour. It sat insolently across one of the lab's most expensive computers. As the Captain approached, it heaved its bulk off the desk and flexed its considerable muscles, an expression on its face that wouldn't have looked out of place on a heavyweight boxer prior to a world championship bout. It let out a honk that sounded like the foghorn on a transatlantic ocean liner.

Captain Schnurrbart didn't miss a beat. In one fluid movement he leapt across a desk and decked the bird with a single punch to the beak. The bird looked astonished for a moment before it staggered, took two steps sideways and crashed unconscious to the floor.

The lab instantly fell silent.

Every goose in the lab stopped moving and looked at Captain Schnurrbart.

'Any of you birds so much as moves a feather and you'll be served up on a platter with potatoes and greens before you can say "honk",' Schnurrbart snarled. 'Now get out of my lab!'

The geese looked rudderless without their leader.

'NOW!' roared Captain Schnurrbart and pointed to the door. The geese knew when they were beaten. With a chorus of muted honks they waddled towards the lab doors. 'Vermorel, Frimmel, DeKooning, Pathfinder! Get these birds locked up in storage room six right away!'

'Yes, sir,' they snapped and began herding the birds out of the lab.

Officer Schmidt loaded the unconscious chief goose onto a small forklift and followed the others. As the last of them left, Hefferning hurried towards the Captain, picking feathers from his uniform and skirting round the larger patches of goose poo that littered the usually clean lab floor.

'Explanation, please, Officer Hefferning,' said Captain Schnurrbart, rubbing his knuckles. 'What were those birds doing in my lab?'

'I'm afraid I don't know, sir,' said Hefferning miserably. 'Frimmel and Vermorel were running a standard infra-red scan on the Duzzent Matter we brought in from the Furcht and the birds just started popping out of nowhere. Before we knew it there were hundreds of them. At first we thought we could handle it ... but, well, we were unsure of how to proceed. Which was when I called you. Sorry, sir.'

Captain Schnurrbart waved his hand.

'No need, Hefferning. You did exactly the right thing. In future, though, if you are faced with wild geese, dominate the leader and they will follow you. Never fails.'

'Yes, sir,' said Hefferning.

Captain Schnurrbart went to where the infra-red spectroscope was housed in a white tube-like container. A narrow window was set into it, through which came a ghostly red light.

'The Duzzent Matter?' said Captain Schnurrbart, nodding at the spectroscope. 'It's still in there?'

'Yes, sir, still inside.'

Captain Schnurrbart bent down to the window, blew a couple of lime-green goose feathers off, and squinted through.

There, under a magnifying prism, sat the tiny speck of Duzzent Matter. It didn't seem like much but, as he peered in, a shiver ran down Captain Schnurrbart's spine. Was it his imagination, or was the thing glowing?

'Let's get this into full quarantine as soon as possible,' he said. 'I don't want things getting any more out of control than they already are. We need to take this silly lump of rock very seriously indeed.'

14

Schnurrbart a traitor?

The information simply refused to sink in. Even after seeing Captain Schnurrbart shoot the cuckoo clock, Sheldon's mind refused to accept the evidence of his own eyes. He dropped into the snow bank and tried to get his breathing under control. Then he looked at The Brain and raised his eyebrows.

The Brain didn't respond. He looked like he was thinking so hard his head might explode.

Meanwhile, Helga was still keeping watch over the snow bank. 'He's going,' she whispered. 'What was *that* all about?'

Sheldon scrabbled upright and peeked over the bank as Schnurrbart disappeared back into the trees. The pyramid was gone. There was no sign of the smaller clocks.

'We need to revise tonight's plan,' said The Brain. 'It's obvious that there's more going at LURV than we can deal with tonight. Agreed?'

Helga and Sheldon nodded. Neither of them was anxious to meet Captain Schnurrbart right now.

The Brain snapped his snowboard into place. 'We'll avoid the road altogether,' he said. 'Should be easier, and downhill all the way.'

He pushed off and slid down the hill.

'Is he going to be OK?' said Helga, watching The Brain disappear down the slope.

Sheldon stepped onto his own snowboard. 'I hope so,' he said. 'He's probably our only remaining option.'

It seemed to take forever to get back to Schnarchen by snowboard. First there was the long board back to the foot of the mountain, then they had to trudge, bone-weary and cold, right across Lucce in time for the first early morning train back to Schnarchen. The winter birds were beginning to chirp by the time they slipped into the house. They sat numbly around the kitchen table, the atmosphere more miserable than a convention of undertakers. The Brain produced his pipe and sat back, arms folded, sucking on it furiously.

'That's an interesting pipe,' said Helga at last, in an effort to lighten the mood.

The Brain took the pipe from between his teeth and looked at it.

'A *meerschaum*,' said Helga. 'Sherlock Holmes's pipe, correct? I always loved those stories!'

'And now you find yourself in one,' said The Brain. 'A mystery as strange as any the great detective was involved in.'

'I suppose I am, aren't I?' said Helga. 'The Curious Case of the Cuckoo Clocks!'

The Brain held the pipe up. 'In fact, this pipe belonged to Sir Arthur Conan Doyle, the creator of Sherlock Holmes. I don't smoke it, of course. I merely use it as an aid to thinking. I find it helps.'

Helga nodded. 'If gets us nearer to finding my father, I'm all for it,' she said. 'Suck it and see if Sir Arthur can come up with any bright ideas.'

Sheldon didn't find the conversation particularly cheering. He stood up. 'Whatever happened out there, we still need to eat and drink. Anyone fancy a hot chocolate? We could do with warming up. Helga? Some chocolate?'

Helga shook her head.

'Coffee,' she said, getting to her feet. 'Strong, black as tar, no sugar. I'll give you a hand.'

'Theo?' said Sheldon.

'Tea, please,' said The Brain. 'Earl Grey, use the china pot if you don't mind, and allow it to stand for precisely two minutes, not a second more, not a second less. No milk, slice of lemon.'

Sheldon and Helga bustled round the kitchen, rustling up the drinks. Helga made a stack of toast and discovered the remains of a shop-bought chicken pie. They placed everything on the table and, under the influence of tea, coffee and toast, the atmosphere slowly began to thaw.

'Any marmalade to go with this toast, old top?' said The Brain.

Before Sheldon could reply, there was the familiar sound of Sheldon's mother coughing awake upstairs. The coughing was the relic of her many years of smoking. Sheldon heard her disappointed groan, the same as every morning, when she reached for her cigarette pack and remembered that she didn't smoke anymore. It was the signal that she was about to come downstairs and fix a cup of coffee—three sugars, full cream, thick enough to stand your spoon up in—a noxious brew that would fell an ox.

Sheldon steeled himself. He had to let his mother know their suspicions about Captain Schnurrbart. It was not going to be a pleasant experience telling her she was married to a moustachioed double-crosser who'd been living a secret life as a psycho clock-shooter. Sheldon would need a lot more hot chocolate to get through the next five minutes. He picked up the kettle and switched on the tap as the kitchen door swung open.

Through it stepped Captain Schnurrbart in his official issue SSSU pyjamas: dark blue with light blue stripes. He sleepily rubbed his thick, non-wriggling moustache.

'Good morning, everyone,' he said, smiling warmly. 'You're up early.' He pointed at their outdoor clothes. 'Going boarding?'

Sheldon froze at the sink, the water overflowing from the kettle.

'Careful,' said Captain Schnurrbart, 'that kettle's full.'

Sheldon blinked and turned off the tap.

'We ... I ... that is, I mean ...' he stuttered.

'We were going to go boarding,' said The Brain, taking Captain Schnurrbart's astonishing appearance in his stride, 'but we changed our minds. We forgot it was a school day.'

Captain Schnurrbart glanced curiously at The Brain. 'You forgot?' he said, putting some sliced bread into the toaster. 'It's not like you to forget.'

The Brain nodded crisply. 'Yes, we forgot. Ridiculous, I know, but there it is.'

Before Captain Schnurrbart could pursue the matter,

the door opened once more and, announced by one last phlegmy cough, Sheldon's mum came in.

'Full house this morning, eh?' she said, looking around the room. 'What's the matter, Sheldon? You seen a ghost or something? You look terrible. Now, where's my coffee? I'm hardly human until I've got a pint or two of good old-fashioned caffeine inside me.'

She reached up and gave Captain Schnurrbart's moustache a loving tickle.

'Morning, Captain,' she said. 'Didn't hear you come back in last night. Not too late, was it?'

Sheldon almost vomited. The sight of his mother canoodling with that ... that clock-shooter, was almost too much to bear. And now he came to think of it, wasn't that moustache the most ridiculous face fungus he'd ever seen?

'Mum!' he barked. 'Don't touch—'

'Don't touch that kettle Mary,' The Brain interrupted. 'It's rather hot.'

'I wasn't going to,' she replied. 'What do you think I am, silly or something?'

She looked at Schnurrbart and rolled her eyes. He shrugged, and thrust his bottom lip out in a gesture that meant 'search me', and began buttering his toast.

'The children do seem a little out of sorts, my dear,' he said kindly. 'Perhaps the events of the past few days have proven too much for them?'

The Brain shot a glance at Sheldon and inclined his head upstairs.

'Yes,' said The Brain. 'That's almost certainly the case, Captain. Too much excitement often has a strange effect on adolescent behaviour. We will take ourselves upstairs and continue our preparations for today's academic studies.'

Watched by the plainly astonished Mr and Mrs McGlone-Schnurrbart, Helga and Sheldon got to their feet.

'Theo is quite right,' said Sheldon. 'We should study. Come on Helga. Let's study.'

Helga smiled apologetically at the McGlone-Schnurrbarts and followed Sheldon out of the kitchen.

'What are you *doing*, Theo?' hissed Sheldon as the kitchen door closed behind them. 'We can't leave Mum down there with that snake! And what was all that stuff about "preparations"? He's bound to be suspicious now.'

'I freely admit, Sheldon, that it was not the smoothest exit I have ever made,' said The Brain, 'but I was thinking on my feet. Something important occurred to me that I wished to have time to examine.'

'What is it, Theo?' said Helga.

The Brain turned into their study and drew them inside. He closed the door and took a seat in one of the big red leather chairs. Helga took the other and Sheldon leaned against the mantelpiece, wishing he too had somewhere to sit. It had been a long night and he was bushed.

'It should have come to me sooner,' said The Brain, shifting in his seat and lifting a magnifying glass from under his bottom. 'I was allowing the visual clues to override the logical ones. How many times have I told you, Sheldon, that when faced with a seemingly insoluble problem one must examine all possibilities, *no matter how unlikely they may be*, before one can make a judgement?'

'Um, quite a few,' said Sheldon, who could feel his eyes

beginning to close. 'In fact, you say it pretty much all the time.'

'We all saw Captain Schnurrbart on the snow, agreed?' The Brain went on.

Helga and Sheldon nodded.

'We all allowed the evidence of our eyes to rule the day. We saw Schnurrbart, so therefore in our minds the person we saw *was* Schnurrbart.'

'What are you saying?' said Helga. She leaned forward excitedly. 'That it *wasn't* Schnurrbart we saw?'

'I'm not sure,' said The Brain. 'An unusual state of mind for me to be in, I can tell you. It may well have been Schnurrbart ... *or someone who in all respects was exactly the same as Captain Schnurrbart.*'

'A doppelganger!' said Helga.

Sheldon looked confused. Which was because he *was* confused. He reached across and pulled up a small cushioned seat.

'A doppelganger is a term that literally means "ghost walker",' said Helga. '*Doppelganger* refers to the appearance, usually ghostly, of an exact double of someone. Of course, now it is more often used when you see someone who simply looks very like someone else.'

The Brain stood up. He rested an arm against the mantelpiece and ran a finger along the teeth of the snarling stuffed mongoose. Sheldon slipped into the vacated chair.

It was good to be sitting down, and he wanted to fall asleep on the spot, but there was something about the doppelganger theory that bothered him. 'Are you saying that there's a killer who happens to look exactly like the

Captain roaming around the Furcht and LURV?' he asked. 'It's a bit far-fetched isn't it? A bit, well, silly?'

'Not quite, old top,' said The Brain. 'I merely put this forward as a theory. It is, of course, still a possibility that the Captain—for some as yet unrealised and no doubt fiendish reason—is a low-down, double dealing scoundrel. Which is why we have to be extremely careful in our actions from this point forward. We must take no chances and, most importantly, we should try and keep this investigation under our control, at least until we are clear about the Captain.'

The Brain yawned, stretched and knocked one of Sheldon's prized bobblehead footy figures off the mantelpiece.

'Hey!' yelled Sheldon, leaping to his feet to catch the falling figure.

The Brain slipped back into the chair with a small smile. He glanced at his watch. 'Now, I suggest we catch a few hours sleep. It has been a tiring night and we have the trip later today. It's already Monday, don't forget.'

'Trip?' said Sheldon. For a moment he wondered if he'd forgotten about a family holiday. He returned the bobblehead to his place on the mantelpiece.

'The school trip, Sheldon,' said The Brain. 'To LURV. I suspect that the answer to our various puzzles lies at LURV. And now I bid you both goodnight. Or, more accurately, good morning. See you in a couple of hours.'

He removed his spectacles, placed them on the arm of the chair and immediately fell fast asleep. One of The Brain's many skills was his ability to fall asleep whenever he wanted, no matter where he was. Another skill was the ability to go without rest for long stretches at a time. During their Australian adventure, he had once remained awake for three days and nights.

'He's right, I guess,' said Helga. 'We should get some sleep too.'

Sheldon nodded. They tiptoed towards The Brain's bedroom, where Helga was staying.

'You know,' Sheldon murmured as Helga opened the door. 'One thing's bothering me about his doppelganger idea.'

'What's that?'

'The clocks,' said Sheldon. 'How on earth does The Brain explain those clocks? Where do they fit into the doppelganger theory?'

Helga shrugged. 'I don't know,' she said. 'There's a lot happened today that needs explaining.'

She lowered her voice and moved closer to Sheldon. For some reason he suddenly found it difficult to breathe.

'And thanks for helping me out when we found the truck,' she said. 'You know, that hand squeezing stuff. I needed that. It was nice. Like you knew how it felt.'

She leaned forward and kissed him on the cheek.

'Goodnight,' she said, and softly closed the door.

Sheldon turned, jumped, and punched the air like a goal-scorer celebrating a last-minute winner. Then he did a silly dance, tucking his hands into his armpits and strutting back and forth like a farmyard rooster.

'Oh yeah, oh yeah, oh yeah, oh yeah!' he chanted softly under his breath. 'Uh-huh! Uh-huh!'

From behind him he heard a cough. He twisted round, hands still tucked under his armpits and one leg lifted in mid-chicken dance. Helga was at the bedroom door watching him, a flicker of a smile playing across her lips.

'Sorry,' she said. 'I thought I heard a noise.'

'Um, yeah,' coughed Sheldon. 'I was just, um ... stretching.' He lifted his arms high above his head and yawned theatrically. 'Yep, stretching. I like to, erm, stretch before going to bed. Relaxes me. You should try it.'

'Oh, OK. Well, goodnight, Sheldon.'

'Goodnight.'

'And Sheldon?'

'Yes?'

'Nice moves.'

The door closed once more. Sheldon groaned and lay down on the floor. He didn't think he'd ever get up.

15

At precisely nine o'clock on Monday morning, the bus left the Ecole for LURV, a journey of about forty minutes. After the incident with Helga, Sheldon had done his best to avoid contact with her. Mainly because he felt there was a risk of his head melting. At least, it felt like it would melt. It certainly got hot enough whenever he remembered her catching him dancing the Funky Chicken. On the bus, he chose the relative safety of a seat next to The Brain.

'Don't you think you should save some food for later?' said The Brain as Sheldon shovelled the last of his packed lunch into his mouth. 'We've only travelled three kilometres.'

'Mnnn-unh,' mumbled Sheldon, shaking his head. 'The best part of school trips is eating your lunch before you arrive. Besides, for all we know, this might be the last food we'll ever eat.'

Fortunately, Sheldon's mother had not had a hand in the food. The Captain had prepared it all. Sheldon wondered for a moment if the Captain might be trying to poison them but decided, after an inspection had revealed some very yummy-looking grub, to risk it. Doppelganger or not, the Captain could certainly rustle up a mean ham sandwich.

Sandwiches swallowed, Sheldon sat back and watched

the snow-streaked countryside flash by. Then he closed his eyes and groaned for the twenty-seventh time that morning as a wave of shame broke over him. That whole dance thing was going to take a bit of getting over. However, although being caught doing the Funky Chicken took some of the shine off the moment but, when all was said and done, *she had kissed him*. And maybe, just maybe, she hadn't really noticed the whole dancing thing?

'Are you all right?' The Brain asked. 'Toothache? Headache? Have you lost something?'

'Only my dignity,' said Sheldon. 'But I'll live. I think.' He changed the subject. 'Any bright ideas since last night?'

The Brain nodded. 'One or two, as a matter of fact, old boy. There were a number of things about yesterday's events that were troubling me.'

'About Schnurrbart?'

'Schnurrbart? Oh yes, of course, Schnurrbart.'

Sheldon frowned. 'You know, I'm not sure, after all that happened up there last night, that I can bring myself to trust the Captain. Even if we what we saw *was* a double-gangler—'

'Doppelganger,' corrected The Brain.

'Doppelganger, whatever. I still think we shouldn't trust him until we find out for sure.'

The Brain looked out of the window.

'No doubt you're right, Sheldon. But I think we're too far into this affair to stop now. And whether or not the Captain is a traitor is meaningless. He will know all about what we do anyway. At least, anything we do above ground.' He pointed up at a distant speck in the sky.

Sheldon leaned across him to look, and saw the distinctive silhouette of the SSSU surveillance helicopter high above the school bus.

'So,' said Sheldon, 'what exactly are we going to do once we get to LURV? I mean we don't have much of a plan. I'm confused.'

'Don't blame yourself, old top. It is confusing. Most confusing. Yet I am beginning to see a shining thread of logic running through the fabric of this case. A thread that I am convinced has its origins in our destination. And, contrary to what you may think, there is a plan for us today.'

'There is?'

The Brain smiled. Only his very close friends (which meant Sheldon) could tell it was a smile. To everyone else it looked like he had something stuck between his back molars.

'Our plan is to have no plan, old boy! We must see whatever we have to see at LURV and make our plans based on the evidence.'

Sheldon leaned back again. The no-plan plan didn't sound like much of a plan to him. He was pretty sure The Brain could have done better.

He risked a glance across the aisle at Helga. She tucked her hands under her armpits and imitated a chicken. Then she smiled and winked.

Sheldon buried his head in his hands.

Three hundred and sixty-two metres below the ground, a truck barrelled along a shaft tunnel running due east from the main Furcht bomb shelter towards the LURV complex.

The tunnel rose on a gradual incline and was wide enough for large vehicles to pass each other without difficulty. This particular truck was gunmetal grey and its powerful engine reverberated deafeningly between the rock faces. Despite the efficient extraction system in the tunnel, the diesel tang of exhaust hung in the air long after the truck had passed.

The driver shifted gears and gunned the engine as the incline grew steeper. Inside the vehicle, two rows of grim-faced individuals sat shoulder to shoulder, bumping and jolting to their destination. There was no conversation. Each of the men wore an identical dark grey uniform and carried a formidable array of weapons, some of which would not have been identifiable by a single weapons-expert on Earth. A quick look into the soldier's eyes would have told anyone that this was not a truckload of office workers making the daily commute.

The man in the passenger seat twisted round and spoke to the uniformed men. 'One minute to arrival,' he snapped. 'No shooting unless absolutely necessary. This will be a holding operation until we hear otherwise. Don't screw any-thing up or there'll be hell to pay from the boss. And we know what that can be like.'

The men nodded. There would be no mistakes.

'Number Two has been monitoring the bus. He's going to meet us and give us a sit-rep before we go in.'

The truck stopped in a wide turning bay and the men dropped to the floor, their boots crunching on the bare rock. They instantly formed into three precise rows of six and stood to attention facing the man issuing their orders.

'Stand easy,' he said. 'We may have to wait for Number Two.'

'Yes, sir!' shouted the men before relaxing their stiff postures. As one, they reached up and absent-mindedly stroked their identical thick black moustaches. It was a gesture that would have been familiar to The Brain and Sheldon, had they been watching. Familiar, because each and every man, including the driver and the man in the passenger seat, was an exact copy of Captain Schnurrbart.

The assembled Schnurrbarts waited patiently in the tunnel. After a few minutes, a figure emerged from the rock wall, passing straight through it like it was water.

'You're late, Number Two,' said the Schnurrbart who seemed to be in command.

Number Two nodded briefly.

'Unavoidable, Number One. The school bus arrived later than expected. They had an unscheduled toilet stop, Number One.'

'All number ones? No number twos at all? That's odd, isn't it?'

'No, Number One, that's not what I meant ... oh, never mind.'

'Do try and concentrate, Number Two. They have now arrived?'

'Affirmative, Number One.'

'Very well,' said Number One with an irritated twitch of his moustache. 'Let's see that these busybodies don't find anything they're not supposed to. Take action if you have to, but remember that the situation is fluid. Things are changing by the second and when the Chief wants us to move in, we'll get the order. Is that clear?'

'Affirmative!' yelled the Schnurrbarts as they snapped to attention.

'Number Two will give you your particular duties once you are inside LURV.'

Number Two nodded and took his place at the head of the Schnurrbarts. 'Let's move it!' he yelled.

'Aye, aye!' bellowed the Schnurrbarts.

They turned as a unit and, weapons held at port arms, ran straight through the rock wall.

Number One turned to the driver.

'Rendezvous here at 1700 hours, Number Nine.'

'I'm Number Six, sir. Number Nine's just left with the others.'

'Number Six, Number Nine!' shouted Number One. 'Whatever your damn number is, you just be here at 1700 hours, is that clear?'

'Yes sir! 1700 it is sir!'

Number Six snapped off a salute and climbed back into his cab. The truck coughed into life, turned sharply away and disappeared down the tunnel in the direction it had come from.

The remaining Schnurrbart took one last look at his watch, adjusted his moustache and followed the rest of the Schnurrbarts through the rock.

16

'It's smaller than I imagined.'

Sheldon, Helga and The Brain stood with the rest of the school party in the visitor entrance at LURV and looked around. They were in a high-ceilinged white lobby dotted here and there with various scientific-looking posters and informational boards that introduced the work taking place at LURV. Sheldon glanced at the one nearest him but got no further than the words 'sub-atomic particle fluctuation modules' before his brain refused to go any further.

'This is merely the above-ground area, old top,' said The Brain.

At first glance, it seemed like The Brain was inspecting the exhibition boards. In fact, Sheldon realised, he was making a mental note of the position and brand of the LURV security cameras.

'Huffmeister,' whispered The Brain, flicking his eyes towards one of them. 'The very best security cameras in the world.'

'Is that a problem?' said Helga.

The Brain shook his head. 'Nothing too difficult. But we may not need to do anything. Let us see how the day unfolds.'

Before Sheldon could compute this information, the two teachers in charge of the trip, Miss Urtl and Herr

Gustaffson, called the class to pay attention. Herr Gustaffson, a music teacher, was a tall, stern, muscular man who seemed uncomfortable in his tweed jacket, and who looked like he'd be more at home wearing the uniform of the SSSU. However, it was Miss Urtl who was the SSSU inside 'man', so to speak. The two teachers stood near a set of double doors with a small man wearing a white lab coat.

'This is Mr Smit,' said Miss Urtl. 'He is to be our guide today around this wonderful scientific facility.'

Mr Smit smiled. His oddly shaped false teeth seemed to have been stuffed haphazardly into his mouth by a dentist with a warped sense of humour. 'Hello, everyone,' he said in a bright voice that would have been more suitable if he'd been talking to a class of four-year-olds. 'I hope you'll have a wonderful and interesting experience here at the Lucce Ultra-Radiation Venture. All we ask is that you follow the tour guidelines and do not stray outside designated areas. This is as much for your own safety as ours. Plus, of course, we do have wild leopards roaming the unauthorised areas.' He grinned hopefully. 'That was a joke. We don't really have leopards. They're panthers.'

The class sniggered politely.

'Yes, well, as I said, just my little, um . . . joke. Now, let's get on with the show shall we? Follow me.'

Smit pushed open the double doors at one end of the room and held them open as the class trooped past.

At first sight, the inside of LURV didn't seem particularly interesting. It resembled a rather dull office building. There were a number of oversized elevator doors facing an open space behind the front office. Smit told them that where they stood was almost a hundred metres above the particle accelerator itself. All of the main business of LURV took place below ground.

'Particle acceleration,' said Smit. 'That's what we do here. We accelerate particles. First I'll explain *how* we do it and then I'll explain *why* we do it!'

Sheldon tried to follow Smit's explanation but, quite frankly, he couldn't. He hadn't really understood it when Helga had explained it the first time. He knew it had something to do with shooting atomic particles round a circular tunnel, but why anyone would want to do that, Sheldon hadn't the foggiest. He filed it in his brain under 'stuff I'll never understand', next to algebra and the rules of cricket.

The Brain was also finding it hard to concentrate, although for quite different reasons. He had learned particle physics as a five-year-old and several experiments of his own had been conducted at CERN, the particle accelerator that LURV had replaced.

After a dull talk about some of the experiments that were taking place at LURV, which went on longer than anyone liked, Smit announced that he'd be taking them down to the main hub of the accelerator.

'The interesting bit!' he beamed.

'At last,' muttered The Brain.

The class crowded into a huge service elevator and Smit pressed the down button. The lift dropped silently for what seemed to Sheldon to be a ridiculously long time before coming to a gentle stop. The doors opened and everyone stepped out.

Smit waved his arms proudly. 'Meet the star of LURV,' he said.

Smit and the school party were dwarfed by the room. One wall was curved, sweeping gently away in either direction in a pure white arc of painted steel. As well as curving away from them, it curved upwards too; Sheldon realised he was looking at one small section of the outside of the accelerator. White-coated workers moved purposefully around the room checking readings on green-glowing monitors. Every sound echoed back from the metallic walls and the air was filled with a low throbbing electricity that seemed to reverberate in the pit of Sheldon's stomach.

It was impressive, Sheldon had to admit, even if he still didn't understand one millionth of what the thing actually did.

Mr Smit stepped across to the curved wall and slapped it.

'Say hello to Pandora,' he said. 'That's our little nickname for this little—or not so little—beauty. Inside this wall, which is one-metre thick, steel-coated, reinforced concrete, is a second, equally strong circular tunnel containing a pulsing "river" of particles that are being accelerated around Pandora's ten kilometre diameter.'

'Is it always operational?' asked The Brain, who already knew the answer.

'A good question, little boy,' said Smit. 'No, Pandora is only operational during experiments. Typically, that might be anything up to twenty times a day. The duration of time she is "on" is dependent upon the experiment being conducted.'

The class followed Smit to a set of steps leading up to a

door that looked like it could cope with a direct hit from a jumbo jet ... which was, in fact, exactly the case.

'Let's take a closer look at Pandora, shall we, children?'

Sheldon looked at Helga who rolled her eyes, impatient to get started.

Smit pressed a code on a keypad next to the massive door. After a momentary pause it swung open smoothly on a steel track and clicked softly into a recess. The class followed Smit inside and found themselves standing in what resembled a portion of a circular tunnel. To one side was a secondary circular tunnel. As in the room they'd just left, the tunnels disappeared in either direction, although inside Pandora it was much more industrial and dirtier-looking than Sheldon had imagined; darker, too, after the brightly lit outer area. The noise level had risen dramatically and Sheldon got a sense of being close to something extremely powerful.

The Brain pointed at Helga's hair, which began to lift gently.

'Magnetic field,' he said. 'Look.'

Sheldon saw that everyone's hair had begun to stand on end. Smit, whose own hair had been plastered down in a pathetic attempt at a comb-over, looked like he had two small black sea anemones clamped to the sides of his head.

'Yes,' he said pressing his hand against his hair in an unsuccessful attempt to keep it under control. 'It's a side-effect of Pandora's magnets. She's absolutely full of magnets!'

He reached out and slapped the smooth outer wall that contained Pandora. 'Go on, touch her!'

Everyone nervously placed a hand against the steel.

Beneath Sheldon's hand it felt like the skin of a great slumbering reptile. It was cold, and his hand throbbed with the magnetised electronic pulses that drove and controlled the whirling particle stream.

'Powerful stuff,' said Helga in his ear. 'Perhaps this is connected with whatever's happened to my dad.'

Sheldon nodded. There was something about the place that was making him jumpy. And it wasn't just Smit's haircut. Feeling the power surge through Pandora he could easily imagine her producing some unbelievable results. But what the connection was with Helga's father, he didn't have the faintest idea.

For lack of anything sensible to say, he jammed his hands back into his pockets. His fingertips rediscovered the raisins from the truck.

'Fancy a raisin?' Sheldon asked Helga, holding out a couple of dusty, lint-flecked raisins. She looked at them and wrinkled her nose.

'Um, very thoughtful of you, but no thanks, Sheldon. Not right now, if that's OK.'

Sheldon moved his hand to his mouth automatically.

'You're not going to eat those?' asked Helga, horrified.

'Oh, er, no,' he said. 'Course not.' Sheldon put them back in his pocket.

'Hey, please don't touch that young man!' said Smit in an even squeakier voice than usual. He scurried across to where The Brain was peering intently at a computer console bolted onto a platform next to Pandora. 'That's an access control for Pandora. We don't want any *accidents* down here, now, do we?'

The Brain regarded Smit icily. Sheldon flinched. Smit didn't stand a chance.

'Then I suggest,' said The Brain, in a tone of solid flint, 'you upgrade your hard drive to one that is made entirely from non-conductive materials, my good man. It is apparent that whatever buffoon put this little excuse for a computer together was unaware of Flimrod Industries's latest hard-drive technology that uses re-constituted carbon-salted plastics to counter the effect of magnetised electronic interference.'

Smit goggled. It was a full five seconds before he managed a reply. 'Yes, well, that is all very well and good. And for your information, *I* am the buffoon who put this computer system together. Now, if we've quite finished these childish games, we can continue with the tour.'

He turned sharply, his lab coat twirling furiously.

'Nice work, Theo,' whispered Sheldon. 'I thought the idea was to keep a low profile and slip away unnoticed? Now that guy is going to remember to keep an eye on you!'

'Precisely, dear boy. I have plans for Mr Smit that require him to be less-than-concerned when I'm not around.'

'Oh, I see,' said Sheldon, although, as usual, he didn't.

Further along the passageway Smit was talking to the class about the next stop, which was the LURV cooling system.

'This is where we get off the tour,' murmured The Brain. He tapped Helga on the arm and pointed at the maintenance door. 'Miss Poom? Shall we?'

Helga checked to see that no-one was looking before nodding briefly.

The Brain inserted a small electronic device he'd constructed from an old iPod into the keypad next to the door. There was a small hiss as the door slid back silently, and the three investigators stepped into the unknown.

17

Captain Schnurrbart walked into SSSU HQ at about the same time that the school bus trip arrived at LURV. He glanced towards the storage area where the geese had been herded and made a mental note to get them moved: the noise was louder than was correct for a top-flight scientific outfit like the SSSU. Captain Schnurrbart saw with disgust he'd got a lump of goose poo on the toe of one of his shiny black boots. He growled and walked into the main control room.

In contrast to the previous night, all was the usual scene of concentrated calm activity. Officers Hefferning, Frimmel, Vermorel, DeKooning, Pathfinder and Schmidt had reported back to work, along with the rest of the SSSU team. Today the alert status was Code Black, the highest level possible.

'Are you sure you should be here, Officer DeKooning?' asked Captain Schnurrbart, pointing to the large bandage wrapped around DeKooning's head.

'Just a flesh wound, sir,' said DeKooning. 'I'm fine.'

'Good. Now can someone give me an update on any developments? Anything to report from the chopper?'

Hefferning pressed a button on his keyboard.

'Observation Chopper One. Sitrep, please.'

There was a small crackle of static and the voice of the

helicopter pilot came through. 'Package arrived safely at target. No unusual activity to report.'

Captain Schnurrbart nodded. 'Good,' he said. 'Remain close by for another ten minutes and then return to base.'

'Affirmative sir,' said the pilot. 'We'll circ—'

Chhhhhhhhhhhz.

The pilot's voice was interrupted by a deafening blast of electronic interference.

'Obs Chopper One!' said Captain Schnurrbart. 'What the devil was that noise?'

'No idea, sir,' said the pilot. 'We had some sort of power surge. The instruments went crazy for a second.'

'Any damage?'

There was a short silence. 'Um, not that I can tell, sir, not to the ship anyway,' said the pilot. 'It's just . . .' He tailed off uncertainly.

'Yes officer? It's just what?'

'Well, sir,' said the chopper pilot, his voice uncertain. 'The helicopter is full of eels.'

'*Eels?*' said Captain Schnurrbart.

'Yes, eels, sir. Slippery, non-finned fish . . .'

'I know what eels are, man!' barked Captain Schnurrbart. 'What I want to know is what they're doing on one of our observation helicopters!'

'They just sort of . . . *appeared*, sir. Right after the power surge. Ugh! One just wriggled across my leg!'

Captain Schnurrbart shook his head. 'Return to base,' he said. 'We'll run some tests. See where they came from.'

'Yes, sir,' said the pilot, and the radio went quiet.

'Eels,' murmured Schnurrbart. 'What is going on?'

'Uh, sir,' said Officer Hefferning pointing to one of the large screens banked against the main wall. 'We've been monitoring local television, sir. This story just came in.'

On screen, a ragged and battered-looking Otto Phleminger was being interviewed. He waved his arms about as he poured out a crazy story about being kidnapped by a flying cow. 'I only just escaped!' he cried, looking right into the camera. 'They tried to eat me! EAT ME!'

Captain Schnurrbart turned to Hefferning. 'A crackpot?'

'Negative, sir,' said Hefferning. 'We've got some radar images coming in of a cow matching Phleminger's description interfering with a flight from Zurich to Rome. The pilot had to take evasive action.' Hefferning walked over to a small table. 'And then there's this, sir.'

'This came from a house three kilometres from LURV. We've analysed it and it is exactly what it looks like. Phleminger's story checks out; there are cows flying around out there. Carnivorous cows.'

Captain Schnurrbart stroked his moustache. 'Anything else?' he asked the room in general. 'Mountains made of marmalade? Pink elephants?'

Officer Vermorel coughed. 'Well, sir, it's a little off base as far as geography goes, but there was a news story on this morning about a contestant in the *Eurovisionara*. Says his trumpet was filled with spaghetti. Might just be a bit of sabotage but . . .'

'Worth monitoring,' said Captain Schnurrbart. 'The way things are going around here, the last thing we need is for the effects to start spreading. Keep an eye on that, Vermorel.'

Officer Frimmel looked up from a computer screen.

'I think I have something else, sir,' he said. 'I've been monitoring local chat rooms and there's been some talk about the banks.'

'Banks?' said Captain Schnurrbart. 'What banks?'

'Well, Swiss banks,' said Frimmel. 'Mainly local banks. There've been reports of some bankers ... um, giving money away.'

Captain Schnurrbart felt the blood drain from his face. He'd have preferred to hear that they had found a mountain made of marmalade. 'Giving money away? This is *Switzerland*! Our banks do not give money away!'

Frimmel nodded. 'It gets worse, sir. Some of the chatters work in local banks. One or two of them are reporting crazy stories about their bank managers turning up dressed, erm, inappropriately.'

'Inappropriately? What do you mean?'

'As Batman, sir. And other superheroes. Spiderman, Superman, that sort of thing. Hans Ledke even came in dressed as Storm from the X-Men; leather cat suit, blonde wig, the works.'

Captain Schnurrbart knew Hans Ledke slightly. He was a portly banker from Lucce with a face like a trout, who specialised in taxation. If a respectable Swiss banker like Ledke was going around dressed in tight-fitting leather and a blonde wig, then something in Switzerland was going very wrong indeed. And Captain Schnurrbart had a pretty clear idea about where all this silliness was coming from.

'The Duzzent Matter,' he murmured. 'Is it ...?'

Officer Vermorel spoke. 'It's safe sir. Safe as safe can be. It's in Q.'

'I need to see it,' said Captain Schnurrbart. 'Right away!'

He strode out of the control room, Vermorel close behind, and headed for the lifts. Far below the main SSSU complex was secure area Q, used mainly for highly toxic chemicals, explosive materials and contagious viruses. It was, thanks to the SSSU top scientists, the most secure place in the world for dangerous substances. After dropping six floors, Captain Schnurrbart left the lift at a jog, swiped his access card through the security reader and, followed by Officer Vermorel, entered Q.

Inside, everything was whisper quiet and antiseptic. The walls of Q were two metres thick and the floor had special built-in anti-earthquake measures. Inside Q was a second, smaller space—though big enough to house an alien space-ship, should another one ever land in Switzerland. Vacuum-sealed and with anti-gravity technology, the atmosphere inside the inner room was basically the same as deep space. Cold, airless, weightless. Whatever was inside Q was supposedly cut off from the rest of the universe.

'You see, sir?' said Vermorel. 'Safe as houses.'

Captain Schnurrbart looked through the thick glass of a viewing port. The black box containing the speck of Duzzent Matter floated motionless in the very centre of the brightly lit room.

'Hmm,' he said.

Captain Schnurrbart turned to Officer Vermorel, a grim expression on his face. 'Get everyone briefed for an imme-diate response, Vermorel. I've a feeling we're going to be needed at LURV sooner rather than later.'

18

They were on their own.

With every passing minute inside LURV, the feeling was growing in Sheldon that they were blundering around as aimlessly, and with as little effect, as a blind man in a hall of mirrors. He had a million questions about the plan—if there *was* a plan—about the cuckoo clocks, and about Captain Schnurrbart's double. Enough questions, anyway, to make him convinced that they were stumbling blindly into a trap.

'I'm seriously worried that we're stumbling blindly into a trap,' said Sheldon, never one to keep his thoughts bottled up.

'Hmm?' said The Brain. 'Did you say something?'

Sheldon shook his head. There was no point in pushing his worries on the others. He wasn't naturally one of those guys who felt good about being in potentially life-threatening situations. Far from it.

They were in what seemed to be a storage area. Cleaning products and various boxes were stacked on metal shelving. The corridor, following the arc of Pandora, curved gently away from them on either side.

'OK, which way now?' asked Helga.

The Brain took out his pipe and tapped the unlit stem against his teeth. He paused for a moment, looking first one way and then another as if weighing up an important decision, before finally pointing his pipe to the left. 'This way. The game's afoot and there's not a minute to lose!'

And with that he jammed his pipe between his teeth and sprinted along the curving corridor.

'How do you know we should go this way?' said Helga as she and Sheldon hurried after him. 'What clues did you pick up on? An atmospheric pressure change? A GPS tracking device concealed in your pipe? How did you know which way the answers are?'

The Brain kept up an impressive pace.

'The answers?' he panted. 'I'm not looking for answers right now, Miss Poom.'

Sheldon shook his head. He didn't understand. 'Then why are we running in this direction?'

The Brain jerked his thumb over his shoulder. 'Because the panthers are in that direction.'

'Panthers?!' said Sheldon. 'What panthers?'

Helga sprinted past Sheldon's right shoulder, picking up speed as she passed him. 'Those panthers!' she yelled, nodding back down the corridor. 'Get moving, Sheldon!'

Sheldon glanced back. Two black shapes were heading towards him, their movements lazy, yet horribly powerful.

Panthers. Real, sleek, dangerous-looking black panthers. Smit hadn't been kidding. Sheldon caught a glimpse of bared white fangs and deep-set glinting eyes. His legs almost buckled as the adrenalin surged through his body.

'We'll never outrun them!' he screamed.

'I'm not trying to outrun them!' yelled The Brain. 'I'm just trying to outrun you two!'

Good point, thought Sheldon as he began to regret

skipping a couple of cross-country runs earlier in the month. Helga was outpacing both him and The Brain, although it was close. It's amazing how fast you can run when there are a couple of panthers chasing you, thought Sheldon.

'I hate black panthers!' yelled Sheldon. 'They look scary!'

'Strictly speaking, they aren't really black,' shouted The Brain. 'Not truly black. They are, more accurately, leopards with a tan; melanistic leopards, to give them their proper name. Their coats have evolved to increase their effectiveness as hunters in dense jungle where little light penetrates.'

'Oh, good!' yelled Sheldon. 'I was worried you were going to tell me something useful. I'm sure I'll feel better knowing I'm being eaten by a melanistic leopard rather than a panther.'

Here, in the brightly lit, white-painted corridor at LURV the panthers stood out like an ink stain on a bed sheet.

'A full-grown black panther has the capability of bringing down a victim that outweighs it by more than three times.' The Brain seemed to be warming to his lecture, despite the pumping of his arms and legs. 'It is also, apart from a few varieties of cheetah, and a few antelope, the fastest land mammal on the planet.'

'Now *that* is something I did not want to know,' yelled Sheldon urging his legs to go faster.

Way ahead of them, Helga looked like she was accustomed to being chased by carnivorous animals every day. Sheldon's panic, in the meantime—never slow to react to stress—had ratcheted up to a complete, total, one hundred percent, maximum setting. He was beginning to wish he was being chased by the cuckoo clock. At least with the clocks he had a fighting chance of escape. Big, fast, sharp-toothed jungle cats were another matter. Quiet though the panthers were, Sheldon would have sworn he could hear the soft thump of their paws as they closed the gap between themselves and their prey. Which, in this case, was himself. What a way to go, thought Sheldon.

Suddenly The Brain skidded to a sharp halt. Sheldon banged into him and the two went sprawling along the floor. Sheldon scrambled to his feet as The Brain stood up and dusted himself off.

'Why did you stop?' yelled Sheldon.

The Brain held up a hand. 'I have a theory,' he said calmly.

Helga, very sensibly in Sheldon's opinion, kept running. She disappeared around a bend in a blur of feet and pumping arms without as much as a backward glance.

It was just Sheldon, The Brain and the panthers.

The big cats slowed as if they knew they could take their prey at any time. They were silent. Sheldon would have preferred a few growls. At least that way he'd be able to judge their mood.

Sheldon clutched at The Brain's sleeve.

'A theory?' he yelped. 'You have a theory? These are flaming panthers! They don't understand your theories, Brain.'

The Brain nodded. 'You are right about that, Sheldon; these creatures do not understand theory. However, while running, I had a chance to examine the available evidence and I am quite certain that we are in no immediate danger.'

'Oh, that's OK, then. We're all safe. Anyone fancy a milk-shake? No? Maybe a nice cup of tea?'

'Stop babbling,' said The Brain. 'Observe.'

He stepped slowly towards the lead panther. It looked angry, and lashed its tail from side to side as The Brain approached. Sheldon could see every sinew of the creature's powerful muscles tense as it crouched ready to pounce.

He hadn't been as scared since the time he'd found a large saltwater crocodile under The Brain's bed. 'I hope you know what you're doing,' said Sheldon, screwing up his eyes. It was too horrible to watch.

The panther made its move. At a speed that Sheldon wouldn't have believed possible if he hadn't seen it himself, the beast sprang through the air, its razor sharp claws extended directly at The Brain's defenceless head. The Brain flinched involuntarily at the moment of impact.

The panther went straight through The Brain.

Sheldon rubbed his eyes as the second panther leapt. It too passed through The Brain's body and landed silently on the other side.

The Brain patted himself down. 'Not a scratch,' he said, his voice wobbling slightly. 'Although I must confess to a slight misgiving just before the moment of truth, so to speak. Still, it is pleasant to be right.'

The panthers looked puzzled. They swung back and forth across the corridor as if trying to make up their minds. Then they both jumped at Sheldon.

He squealed as, fangs bared, the panthers came directly at him; then closed his eyes as they passed through him and landed on the floor behind him.

'I don't understand,' said Sheldon, feverishly examining his body for damage. 'How is that possible? Are these things, what, like holograms or something?'

'Not holograms,' said The Brain. 'These *are* panthers; or at least creatures that look very like panthers. But I knew they would be unable to harm us. What organisation, no matter how strange, would allow wild panthers to roam its premises? This *is* Switzerland, after all.'

Sheldon looked down to see a panther trying unsuccessfully to eat his leg. It was the oddest experience to watch a large jungle cat seemingly biting through flesh and bone without feeling any pain. Sheldon shook his leg. The panther gave up and slunk across to its partner.

'I thought you say this was easy, Hector,' said the panther who'd been trying to chew Sheldon. It spoke in a strong South American accent. 'Just run the gringos down and eat, you said; no trouble, you said, yes?'

'Hey, don' blame me, man,' said the second panther. 'How was I to know they gonna be some more of those weird, non-eatin' type gringos? You see a label on their butt, or somethin'? No, I do not think so, Ruben, I do not think so!'

'Man, I know. I hate this place!'

'Me too, *viejo amigo*. It sucks! Less go bro.'

The panthers sloped away down the tunnel, shoulders drooping.

'They talk?' said Sheldon. 'Talking panthers?'

'It's very difficult,' said The Brain, 'for someone of your intelligence to understand what's happening. I have begun to piece a few threads of this mystery together and it's hard enough for me. As far as the panthers are concerned, we do not quite have the full tapestry in front of us, but I *was* fairly sure that whoever is behind this did not want us to be eaten.' He looked up at a security camera that Sheldon hadn't noticed before and spoke directly at it. 'Isn't that right, Professor Weiss?'

There was an electronic click and a voice came over a loudspeaker. 'Bravo, Mr Brain! Bravo! I think it's time we met. Stokes will show you to my office.'

They heard the sound of soft hand claps mixed with a deep bass chuckle. A nearby door slid open to reveal an English butler in formal buttling clothes. He looked exactly like you'd imagine a proper butler to look, except that he had two heads.

'Good morning, gentlemen,' said one of his heads in a London accent.

'If you'd like to follow me,' said the other.

'After you, Sheldon,' said The Brain and they stepped through the door. 'It's time to meet the Professor.'

19

The two-headed butler padded softly along the thickly carpeted corridor. The Brain and Sheldon followed a few paces behind.

'He's got two heads,' whispered Sheldon.

The Brain raised an eyebrow. 'Yes, I noticed.'

'I know you noticed. What I mean is, *how* has he got two heads? What's going on down here? The whole place is like some sort of freak show!'

The Brain nodded. 'It would appear so, old top. Perhaps the Professor may be the person to shed some light on it.'

'Who is he, this professor?'

The Brain took a thoughtful suck on his unlit pipe. 'Weiss is probably—no, not probably—Weiss *is* the world's leading scientific expert on particles. There's nothing really worth knowing about particles that Weiss does not know. That said, there's an awful lot of things about particles that no-one knows anything about. Not even me.' He jabbed the end of his pipe at Stokes's back. 'But seeing Stokes and the panthers, not to mention our encounter with the clocks, makes me wonder if the professor knows the most important thing about particles.'

'And what's that?'

'When you play with matches, don't be surprised if you burn down the house.'

Before Sheldon could ask what The Brain meant, Stokes slid to a halt outside a wooden door and tapped softly. Then he opened it and gestured for them to step inside. 'If you'd like to enter, gents, the Professor will see you now.'

For a brief moment, Sheldon wondered if they had passed through some sort of time portal. The clean, antiseptic feel of the corridor had not prepared him for Professor Weiss's office. It was like stepping into a conservatory furnished sometime during the 1890s. Thick, richly patterned Indian rugs covered a black-and-white tiled floor. Heavy, old-fashioned, wooden furniture filled the room, jostling for position with a thick jungle of hothouse plants. Foliage, vines, creepers, tendrils of tropical flora hung down from the unseen ceiling. Exotic orchids sat in deep ceramic pots, their luxuriant leaves beaded with moisture. The atmosphere was stifling. Despite there being no windows, the place seemed dappled in sunlight. Sheldon looked up and glimpsed two banks of powerful hydroponic lamps shining through the foliage. The place was an exotic greenhouse.

Stokes raised a hand to one of his mouths and coughed a low, buttling sort of cough, the kind Sheldon imagined they taught only at the highest quality butler schools.

From amongst the foliage came a deep voice.

'Please, come.'

Stokes nodded one of his heads and gestured for Sheldon and The Brain to follow him. 'This way, gents. Mind the *flarze.*'

Sheldon glanced at The Brain.

'He means "flowers",' whispered The Brain.

The three zig-zagged between a couple of over-sized potted ferns and, after Stokes brushed aside some hanging vegetation from their path, they found their host sitting behind a huge mahogany desk that could have doubled as a landing strip on an aircraft carrier. His head was bent over a laptop. A bright green-and-red parrot sat on a gilded perch behind his right shoulder, chewing on a large seed. It bleakly surveyed the new arrivals out of one beady eye. The parrot had the air of a bird that had seen plenty and, on the whole, didn't like it much.

'Begging your pardon, sir, but the two young gentlemen what you asked for is here,' announced Stokes.

The Professor raised his head. 'Excellent. Thank you, Stokes. That will be all.'

'Very good, sir,' said Stokes, sliding from view.

The Professor was a massive lump of a man, a brown-skinned mountain of flesh wrapped in a beautifully made, three-piece suit of white velvet that must have used up most of the world's white velvet supply. The tailor had done wonders with the cut of the material, turning Professor Weiss into a merely fat man, rather than the astonishingly obese tub of lard he actually was.

A constant river of sweat poured from his brow. He mopped and dabbed at his face with a lavender-scented purple silk handkerchief the size of a parachute. Although almost bald on top, he wore what remained of his tightly curled, wet-looking hair pulled back in a ponytail, tied with what resembled a diamond-encrusted scrunchie. He wore a thin goatee that curled around the chin nearest to his mouth.

But his physical appearance, though strikingly unusual, was not the strangest thing about him. The most memorable thing, which everyone who met him remembered, was his voice.

'Why, hello there, fellers,' he boomed in a rich, deep voice that rolled out across the room and flowed into Sheldon's ears like warm honey. 'Lemme introduce myself. Professor Eugene Carter Weiss, the doctor of LURV at your service. If you're partial to a particle, or particular about a proton, then you need some LURV in your life! Heh, heh, heh. Just my l'il joke, there.'

He struggled forward for a few moments, his flesh wobbling under the white velvet with the strain of getting out of his chair. Finally he gave up and sank back. He mopped his brow. 'Y'all will have to excuse *moi* for not getting up to greet you like a proper Texan gentleman. The problem is my diet, you see. I don't have one! Heh, heh, heh, heh!'

'Delighted to meet you, Professor Weiss,' said The Brain leaning across the desk to shake the Professor's enormous paw. 'I have long been an admirer of your work on overcoming synchrotonic radiation loss, to say nothing of your groundbreaking work with strange quarks and super-symmetric particles.'

Professor Weiss beamed. 'Why thank you so much, Theo. It is rare indeed to find someone of your age so downright funky about the world of particle acceleration, uh-huh!'

The parrot screeched, and Sheldon jumped.

'Little bleeders! Nasty BEEPING boys! Walk the BEEPING plank! Keelhaul 'em!'

Professor Weiss shook his head. 'Ah'm sorry about Otis,'

he said. 'He gets overexcited at times. Used to belong to a seafaring gentleman and his language is not always as classy as ah would like.'

'You BEEPING BEEP BEEPS!' said the parrot.

'Oh my!' said Professor Weiss. 'Now that's bad, even for Otis.' He opened a desk drawer and gave Otis a walnut. The bird took it and stopped squawking.

'That's better,' said Professor Weiss, sitting back. 'Now that we have some peace you can tell me just why it is that you are here at LURV. Is it simple curiosity, or does the good Captain Schnurrbart have something to do with your "school trip"?'

He raised a quizzical eyebrow. The effort involved caused a fresh crop of sweat to break out on his forehead. He dabbed at them with his sopping handkerchief.

'The Captain does know about the trip,' said The Brain. 'I knew it was unlikely to have escaped your attention. Still, a school trip was the best we could come up with at short notice. Events have been unravelling at some speed since you made your breakthrough.'

The Professor's smile vanished. 'Breakthrough? What do you mean "breakthrough"?'

'Come, come, Professor Weiss. There's no need for modesty. It has been obvious to me for some time that you have recently made some sort of breakthrough with the work here.'

The Professor's eyes, buried deep in the flesh of his face like diamonds in the mud, glittered excitedly. He looked like someone with a wonderful secret that he was dying to tell everyone about.

'I can see I have underestimated you,' he boomed. 'You are right, of course. We have had a bunch of success with our latest experiment in Pandora. Quite remarkable results. It's not too much to claim that it's the greatest scientific discovery since Newton got beamed by that apple!'

The Brain leaned forward. 'Let me guess,' he said. 'Dark matter?'

The Professor nodded and his face lit up like a kid's face at Christmas. A diamond set into one of his teeth caught the light. 'We found it, Theo! We found it! And it's *more*, so *much* more than we had hoped for! We can find the answers now; the Big Bang, the Big Crunch, the Big Rip, the multi-verse, the whole shooting match laid out for us!'

The big man held his hand to his chest as if feeling faint. 'Ah'm sorry for getting so excited, boys. But if you knew what I know now . . .'

'And the Duzzent Matter?' said The Brain. 'How long have you been tinkering with that little item?'

Professor Weiss looked puzzled. 'Duzzent Matter? I'm afraid you have me at a disadvantage, young man. I'm not familiar with this term. Brown Dwarfs, Red Dwarfs, Quarks, Black Holes . . . but Duzzent Matter is not something I've had the pleasure of working with.'

The Brain glanced at Sheldon. 'It's worse than I thought,' he murmured, then turned back to Professor Weiss. 'Perhaps you could show us some of your developments, Professor?'

'Why not?' beamed Professor Weiss. It was obvious he was dying to show someone his new train set. He heaved himself upwards, sank back down, lurched forward and teetered on the edge before achieving enough upward motion to lift himself to his feet.

Sheldon breathed a sigh of relief. He didn't fancy giving the Professor a hand up. Or CPR.

The Professor stood panting for a moment. Alongside his desk was a specially reinforced electric scooter. With some effort Weiss stepped onto the footplate and pressed a button on the controls. The machine groaned into life and Weiss rolled towards the door, weaving between the potted plants.

'We need to check in on Pandora anyway!' he shouted as he buzzed across the floor. 'Let's roll!'

'Stuffin' BEEEPY BEEP BEEPS!' screeched Otis.

Sheldon blinked. That bird could swear, no doubt about it. Sheldon passed the potty-mouthed parrot another walnut and followed The Brain towards the door.

'Good riddance, bumface!' screeched Otis through a beakful of walnut.

Outside Professor Weiss's office Sheldon tugged at The Brain's sleeve. 'What's happening? Where are we going now?'

'I'm not entirely sure of the details, old top. Not yet, anyway,' said The Brain, as he walked after Professor Weiss's receding bulk. 'But I do know one thing: we're going to have a hell of a time putting the genie back into that lamp.'

20

They followed Professor Weiss's protesting scooter through a maze of corridors and work spaces, past gleaming laboratories and dark, mysterious industrial areas. Great looping garlands of thick black electrical cables hung down from the roof. Ducts and pipes wove in and out of each other in a dizzying spaghetti of metal and plastic. Everywhere, the constant background hum of electricity filled the air.

Eventually they arrived at the control room. Professor Weiss keyed in a code and pressed his hand against a glowing LED display screen.

'ID confirmed,' said a metallic voice.

The door slid open and Sheldon and The Brain followed the Professor into another long curving room that followed the contours of the particle accelerator. Here the electrical hum was stronger than anywhere else in LURV. Sheldon could almost feel his skin vibrating. An entire wall was filled with blinking panels of sleek-looking electronic equipment. There was an air of total calm and purpose in the room. An LED display on a nearby wall told Sheldon the temperature was carefully controlled at a perfect twenty-five degrees. Despite this, he shivered.

A couple of workers wearing white lab coats looked up from their computer screens and nodded to the Professor as his scooter slid towards them.

'Morning, boys,' said Professor Weiss. 'How's my baby doing today?'

The worker nearest to Weiss tapped a couple of keys on his console and glanced at the screen before replying. 'Pandora's operating at twenty-two percent capacity, Professor. We have the Japanese team experiment starting on Thursday and we're trying to clean up those, um, fluctuation readings we've been getting.'

'Fluctuation readings?' said The Brain. 'Are you getting readings you can't explain?'

The Professor waved a meaty paw. 'Nothing important. Merely some spikes in the particle flow: blips, glitches, teething problems.'

The Brain pushed his glasses up his nose and fixed a beady stare on Professor Weiss. As beady stares go, it was one of the beadiest. 'Let me make a guess, Professor. Those "teething problems" that Pandora is having started not long after you discovered the dark matter?'

The laboratory worker looked up. 'Why, yes! How ...'

Professor Weiss gestured to him to stop talking. 'A coincidence, is all,' purred the Professor. 'Nothing of any real concern.'

The Brain took out his pipe and placed it between his teeth. Sheldon knew The Brain was thinking as fast as he was capable (which was pretty fast). He kept studying the computer screen, but spoke urgently to the Professor. 'And these "coincidences" also happened to coincide with the appearance of Stokes, the panthers and the cuckoo clocks?'

'Cuckoo clocks?' said Professor Weiss. 'What do you mean, cuckoo clocks?'

Unlike most people, when The Brain wanted to make his point more clearly, he lowered his voice. 'You are meddling with forces much greater than you can possibly imagine, Professor,' he said softly. 'It is not too much of a claim to say that the fate of Switzerland rests upon what happens in the next few hours at LURV.'

Professor Weiss shook his head and growled out a laugh that reminded Sheldon of the rumble of traffic. 'Jumpin' Jehosophat!' he said. 'What superstition! We're men of science here! I had thought that y'all would see our magnificent achievements for what they were!'

He dabbed at his forehead with his handkerchief.

'The achievement is unquestionable,' said The Brain. 'I am in complete agreement with that. However, I really do not think you understand the consequences of what has happened. You do *not* have control of events. They clearly have control of you, and you—all of us—are in dire peril unless we close down Pandora immediately. It is the only option!'

Professor Weiss threw his head back and laughed again. 'Close Pandora down? What a ridiculous idea. Pandora is the greatest scientific achievement of our—of *any*—century!'

He stopped talking and gave The Brain a kindly look. The sort you'd give when talking to an elderly relative who thought he was the Emperor of Japan, and had taken to wandering around in his underwear.

'Look,' said the Professor, 'I can see that this has all been something of a shock to y'all. It's only to be expected, I suppose, even when someone with your scientific abilities is confronted by the concept of the multiverse.' He placed a hand on The Brain's shoulder. 'Let me show you what Pandora can do. Then I'm sure you'll be convinced. How does that sound?'

The Brain nodded. 'Very well, Professor. Perhaps you're right. It is possible that my assistant and I have been some-what overexcited in our assessment of the situation.'

'Well, alright!' said Weiss. He scooted towards the main computer console and slapped the operator on the back.

'Fire her up, boys! Let's show our guests just what Pandora is capable of!'

He bent down closer to the computer operator, his eyes gleaming, and began to discuss technicalities.

Sheldon glared at The Brain. 'What are you doing?' he hissed. 'You need to tell them about the truck and the Schnurrbarts . . . all that stuff! It's got to be connected with all this going on here.'

The Brain shook his head. 'I do not believe the good Professor is in any mood to hear what he believes are idiotic theories,' he whispered. 'I think we must play along until— *if*—we can spot an opportunity to close down Pandora ourselves. The fool does not even know he has produced Duzzent Matter. Since Pandora is the only possible source of Duzzent Matter, it is of the utmost urgency that we find a way to stop it.'

Sheldon shrugged.

'If you say so. I just, I don't know, I guess I'm getting more than a little worried about little things like, you know, being chased by panthers, two-headed butlers, that sort of thing.'

'It's all the same thing, old top, don't you see? Pandora is the source. But we must tread carefully. We do not want to enrage the misguided Professor and lose our access to the heart of the problem. Some tact is required.'

Sheldon nodded and then blinked as he remembered something. 'What about Helga?' he said. 'Where is she?'

The Brain paused. 'I am sure that she's fine. Miss Poom is made of pretty durable material.'

Sheldon made a face. 'I hope you're right, Brain.'

21

Helga leaned on a steel railing that ran round the maintenance walkway directly above the particle accelerator and tried to get her breath back. Beneath her feet she felt the throb of Pandora's powerful magnetic field. Her hair blew gently in the warm, dry breeze that flowed steadily through the tunnel.

It had been a near thing with the panthers. She had barged through door after door and ended up where she now was, hopelessly lost.

The walkway extended right around Pandora, servicing the circular inspection hatchways that had been built into the accelerator every two hundred metres. At each inspection point, other metal walkways led off towards different sections of the LURV complex. It was on one of these inspection points that Helga now stood. She had to try and get her bearings, make her way back to the main complex, find The Brain and Sheldon, and see if—

From somewhere up ahead, footsteps rang out. They seemed to be coming in Helga's direction. Then, about fifty metres away, a shadowy figure strode out of the gloom towards her. Her first thought was relief. If this was a maintenance worker, or a laboratory assistant or someone like that, she'd be safe. She opened her mouth to call out.

Then some survival instinct stopped the cry in her throat.

She remembered The Brain's conviction that her father's disappearance was linked with something at LURV. And something about the approaching figure's way of walking told her this wasn't a friendly maintenance crew member.

She drew back into the shadow and looked round for a hiding place.

Then there was another sound. More footsteps, this time from behind her.

Helga was trapped on the walkway.

She dropped to her knees and held her breath. Silently, she slid over the edge of the rail and wedged herself in an inky patch of shadow between a girder and the underside of the walkway. She made herself as small as possible.

Above her, the footsteps drew nearer until they clanged heavily onto the steel above her head. Through the walkway mesh she could only catch fleeting glimpses of the figure moving against the dim strip-light.

'Number One,' said a voice. 'You're late.'

Helga recognised the voice and almost fell from her hiding spot. The new arrival was Captain Schnurrbart.

Or his doppelganger.

'Apologies, Chief,' said Number One as he snapped off a crisp salute and stood to attention. 'The complex is more complex than I thought.'

The man called Chief moved closer to Number One.

'I'm surrounded by imbeciles!' The words were spat out in such a fury that Number One took a step backwards. 'I ought to fry that idiot Number Two!' the Chief continued. 'Do you know he let some of the multiverse creatures loose up top? Anything could have happened! How many times have I told you that secrecy is of the essence? It's bad enough that we're getting leakage as it is.'

He took a deep breath and drummed his fingers impatiently on the rail. 'The others? Where are they? It's time to assume control and get our program back on track!'

Captain Schnurrbart's double clicked his fingers once. For a moment nothing happened. Then, silently, eighteen Captain Schnurrbarts materialised through a wall below the walkway. For a second time, Helga almost fell. She jammed her fist against her teeth to stop herself crying out. If one of them so much as glanced in her direction she'd be undone. Helga sensed, rather than saw, the one they called Chief step towards the rail and look down at the assembled Schnurrbarts.

'Events have moved more quickly than even I anticipated. Pandora needs to be under our full control soon or we will begin to attract more unwanted attention from the meddling SSSU. That jumped-up Brain idiot and his feeble-minded monkey have, somehow, located the truck. It has directed them in our direction, although, thankfully, they seem to be clueless about our purpose. It's time to act; time to put the plan into operation. Shoot on sight. Spare no-one.'

'Aye, aye, sir!' shouted the Schnurrbarts.

The Chief turned to Schnurrbart Number One.

'See that it's done,' he said, and went away along the walkway.

Number One leapt easily over the rail and joined his platoon. 'You heard him,' he said. 'Let's get moving!'

They melted through the wall and Helga was alone.

She needed to find The Brain.

22

Professor Weiss straightened up from the computer console with difficulty. He dabbed his forehead with his handkerchief and beamed at Sheldon and The Brain.

'Pandora is a gateway to an alternate universe, young man!' said Professor Weiss. 'We can use her to go, well ... anywhere!'

The Brain looked at Weiss. 'But you have no control over where you go, is that correct?'

'Well, yes.'

'And that's where Stokes and the panthers came from? From Pandora, during one of these power surges?'

Weiss beamed. 'Exactly. We were so excited when Stokes arrived! He has been so useful to us. Of course we have no way, yet, of returning him but, thankfully, so far he seems quite content. And he makes an excellent butler.'

'I must advise you, Professor, that this discovery, this access to other universes, scientifically interesting though it is, should be destroyed before it destroys us. That is, unless it's already too late.'

'Nonsense! We take the utmost care in controlling it. We have things very secure down here you know?'

The Brain shook his head. 'Really?' he said, his voice acid. 'Then perhaps it would interest you to know that someone else has access to Pandora's secrets? Has developed multiverser *weapons*? And that other crossovers are happening already? This technology is not under your control; it has *you* under *its* control!'

Weiss licked his lips. 'I'm sure that there's a perfectly reasonable explanation for any, um, glitches, that may have happened—'

'These are not "glitches" Professor,' The Brain interrupted. 'Someone, or something, is using Pandora's secrets for their own fiendish ends.'

The control room had fallen silent as the discussion continued.

'I think I've heard enough,' said Weiss. 'It is clear, sadly, that you do not possess the same vision as I. Now, if you would be so kind as to return to the school party. I think our business here is done.' He motioned The Brain and Sheldon out of the room. 'You'll find your way back by following the exit signs. Now, I have important work to do. Good day.'

He closed the main control room door.

'Well, I think that went very well,' said Sheldon. 'Don't you?'

The Brain paced up and down the corridor for a minute or two. He placed his pipe between his teeth and hummed a few bars of a popular song. As he paced, the floor seemed to vibrate slightly and Sheldon felt the hairs on the back of his neck stand up.

'A power surge,' he said. 'Shouldn't we, like, worry about that? Isn't that when, y'know, weird stuff happens?'

The Brain didn't reply. He tapped his pipe against his teeth.

'Um,' said Sheldon, holding up a finger. 'You do know

that it's, like, the end of the universe or something pretty soon? Not that I'm worried or anything you understand. Feel free to think all you like.'

'Thank you, Sheldon.'

It was all Sheldon could do to not to pick up a fire extinguisher and let The Brain have it right between the eyes. Thinking was all well and good (and no-one did thinking better than The Brain did thinking), but he'd have liked to see a bit less *thinking*, and a lot more *action*. Couldn't The Brain sense that things were getting weirder by the minute? That power surge, for example.

'Come on,' said The Brain. 'We haven't got time to stand around, you know. I need to speak to the Professor again.'

Sheldon ground his teeth. He found it helped sometimes.

The main control room was hushed as they stepped back inside. Immediately, both of them felt something had changed. The soft electronic hum of expensive scientific instruments was the only sound. No murmur of workplace chatter, no slurping of coffee, nothing.

Not only that, but the control room was completely empty. Professor Weiss's scooter stood idle.

'Professor?' said The Brain. 'Professor Weiss?

'No-one here. Oh, well,' said Sheldon, whose nervous system was dancing a tango. 'No sense in hanging around eh? C'mon, let's go.'

The Brain raised a hand.

'Silence, dear boy. Try and remain calm. I'm sure there is a perfectly logical explanation for Professor Weiss's absence.'

'Maybe the panthers discovered the secret of eating?' suggested Sheldon. 'Or a pack of rabid wolverines, maybe?'

'There are no wolverines in Switzerland, Sheldon. At least, none from our universe. Now please settle yourself and allow me to do what I do best: investigate.'

Sheldon's shoulders slumped. Once the Brain had his teeth into a problem there was no letting go until it was resolved. And this was a thorny problem. They'd been with Professor Weiss only minutes previously. From what Sheldon could see there were no other exits, yet clearly the Professor and the control room workers had vanished.

'Maybe they're hiding behind the computer?' Sheldon said, pointing at a computer stack the size of a small filing cabinet.

'Or possibly they have stowed themselves inside the waste paper basket? Or it could be that they've fallen down the back of that chair?' said The Brain, shaking his head.

Sheldon moved across to the waste paper basket and peered inside. The Brain looked at him strangely. 'What *are* you doing?'

'I was just checking. You said—'

'I was being sarcastic. You know sometimes I begin to wonder about my choice of you as—'

The Brain broke off suddenly and he too looked into the waste basket.

'Good grief,' he said and produced a small, high-powered magnifying glass. 'Sometimes you do surprise me, old bean.'

'Yes, well,' said Sheldon huffily. 'There's no need for insults, *old bean*. Even I know the Professor isn't in the bin.

I just thought there might be, y'know, a clue or … something.' He tailed off limply.

'Yes, quite,' said The Brain. 'Now please be a good chap and keep quiet for a moment. This could be quite delicate.'

The Brain produced a minute pair of tweezers. He reached slowly into the wastepaper basket and, with infinite care, picked up a small object. Grabbing a sheet of paper from a nearby desktop printer, he laid it flat on the desk and dropped the tiny object onto the centre.

Sheldon screwed up his eyes and looked closely. On the paper was a wrinkled raisin, black and purple in colour. It looked old, and dry as dust, as if it had been in the bin for some time.

'A raisin?' said Sheldon. 'What's so special about a mouldy old raisin?'

'Look closer,' said The Brain.

He handed Sheldon the glass. Sheldon put it to his eye and bent closer to the raisin. It took a while to focus. Eventually he found the right distance and he saw what was on the paper. In every detail. He gasped and almost dropped the magnifying glass.

'That's impossible!' he jabbered. 'That's just … *impossible!*'

'Yes,' said The Brain, 'it *is* impossible, yet nevertheless there is the evidence in front of us. That's no raisin …'

23

After a glass of water from a nearby cooler, Sheldon felt a little better. Not calm, exactly, but well enough to start coming to terms with what he'd seen. The old raisin, when looked at through The Brain's glass, was not a raisin.

It was the tiny shrivelled figure of Professor Eugene Carter Weiss.

If you looked carefully, really carefully, you could just about make out his goatee beard on his dried-out, wrinkled little face.

After a few minutes searching underneath chairs and on the floor, The Brain found the shrunken remains of the rest of the control room workers. He placed them side by side on the sheet of paper and inspected them thoughtfully.

Sheldon couldn't take his eyes off the little raisins. It was an effort to remember that just a few minutes ago they had all been fully functioning humans. Now they looked like something a fussy eater had picked out of a bowl of muesli.

The Brain was still staring thoughtfully at the shrivelled-up little raisin bodies. 'Um, Sheldon?' he suddenly murmured.

'Yes?' said Sheldon, his voice still quavery. 'What is it?'

'You remember the truck in the Furcht tunnel?'

Sheldon nodded. 'Yes.'

'Did you eat anything from that cab?'

'Well, um, I found a loose raisin on the seat of the cab and I, um, well, I . . . ate it.'

The Brain looked even more thoughtful. 'Was it a chocolate raisin by any chance?'

Sheldon shook his head. 'No, a regular raisin. A pretty dry one too.'

'Ah,' said The Brain.

'*Ah*?' said Sheldon. In his experience, when someone said 'ah' it usually meant that either something bad was about to happen, or a spot of bad news was about to be delivered. He was right.

'Yes, Sheldon, "*ah*". You see, the scrunched up bag in the cab *was* a bag of chocolate raisins. The one you foolishly ate was not.'

'You don't mean . . .?' said Sheldon, the blood draining from his face.

'I'm afraid so, old boy,' said The Brain sadly. 'You ate Helga's father.'

Medical experts will tell you that vomiting is controlled, or directed, by a part of the brain known as the lateral medullary reticular formation. Sheldon's lateral medullary reticular formation must have gone into meltdown because, on hearing that he'd eaten the father of the most beautiful girl to walk the face of the earth, he puked all over an expensive laptop, a desktop seismic monitor, a discarded cup of latte, two workstation desks, a couple of chairs, a wastebasket and parts of The Brain's shoes. Once he'd finished he put his head down on a non-puke covered part of a desk and moaned miserably. Eating a girl's father was probably not the way to her heart.

The Brain wiped the vomit from his shoes with a tissue from a box on the desk and patted Sheldon softly on the back.

'Look on the bright side,' he said. 'At least we found him.'

Sheldon moaned again. How would he ever explain this to Helga? 'Sorry, O girl of my dreams, I've got some good news and some bad news. The good news is that we tracked down your dad. The bad news is that I polished him off as a light snack.'

It wouldn't go down well. Unlike Mr Poom.

The Brain hauled Sheldon to his feet. 'We must move on, old thing.'

Sheldon nodded miserably. 'I suppose so,' he said. He wiped his face with his sleeve and looked down at what was left of Professor Weiss. 'What happened to these guys?'

The Brain tapped the mouthpiece of his pipe against his teeth. 'After everything that has been happening, I am not altogether surprised to find something like this. The fool was meddling with powers beyond his comprehension. The big question is: has Weiss opened up a gateway to an uncontrolled and uncontrollable universe of silliness? The Professor and his team have been literally playing with fire. Once Duzzent Matter is out in the world, anything goes. Holes in cheese sandwiches disappear. Trucks get embedded in solid rock. Panthers and two-headed butlers cross over from alternative universes. Basically, anything that could happen in any one of an infinite number of possible universes, may happen.' The Brain paused. 'For instance, *we* may be about to be turned into raisins ourselves. I have no way of knowing. It could be that the Duzzent Matter operates in "pulses". There may have been one such pulse when we were outside the room.'

'Something did happen!' said Sheldon. 'One of those pulse things! While we were outside in the corridor the floor shook!'

The Brain nodded. 'Quite possibly. On the other hand, I suspect that something else completely is behind what's happening here. Some*one*, in fact. And I have my suspicions about who that might be.'

'Well? Who?' asked Sheldon. 'And shouldn't we be getting out of here before we get, y'know, raisined or something?'

Before The Brain could answer, a searing bolt of bright light smashed into a computer next to them. The computer disappeared and was replaced instantaneously by a puzzled-looking creature that resembled a tiny purple-and-orange-spotted whale.

There was no time to wonder what it was or what was happening. Sheldon and The Brain dived behind a metal workstation as the creature jumped to the ground and flapped awkwardly across the control room floor.

Another blast of light hit the wall behind them and that part of the wall became a sheet of glowing blue ice. The Brain hunkered down and peeked around the edge of the desk. Sheldon did the same and immediately wished he hadn't.

24

Three Captain Schnurrbarts were inside the control room. All carried snub-nosed weapons, and all looked like they knew how to use them. Worse still, they looked like they *wanted* to use them, preferably sooner rather than later.

The Brain scanned the situation. Behind them a solid wall. Ahead, the Schnurrbarts. No chance of escape left or right.

'What are we gonna *do*, Brain?' Sheldon was watching the whale creature make its way awkwardly towards a nearby filing cabinet. 'I don't wanna be turned into one of those *things!*'

Before The Brain could reply, another blast of light hit the desk they were sheltering behind. It was instantly replaced by six aggressive looking humanoid tribesmen painted from head to toe in red dye and carrying odd-looking curved spears. These they shook in fury at the Schnurrbarts. The Schnurrbarts paused for a moment. One of the warriors looked down at The Brain and Sheldon and howled at them in a language Sheldon doubted had ever been heard on Earth. He raised his spear and Sheldon flinched.

Another blast from a Schnurrbart gun hit the wall, turning it into a section of gently waving grass. The Brain didn't hesitate. Seizing Sheldon, he hurled them both through the grass and they rolled into a brightly lit corridor, a spear thudding into the corridor wall opposite.

Up. Running. Don't look back. Don't hesitate. Hesitation means being turned into a purple and orange whale, or an alien tribesman, or grass, or ice, or *something*.

Sheldon felt, rather than heard, more blips of light from the guns. A water cooler morphed into a waxy pile of green gunge, a fire extinguisher turned into a man wearing Victorian-style clothes sitting on a bicycle. Sheldon would have thought the expression on his face was funny if he hadn't been running for his life.

The Brain rounded the corner a fraction ahead of Sheldon. He saw a maintenance doorway. Sheldon lurched towards it as The Brain pulled it open. But before he could dive through, The Brain pulled him back and nodded instead towards a large LURV laundry trolley standing opposite the door. Sheldon understood. The Urtl Shoelace Manoeuvre. Or something like it. Misdirection was one of Miss Urtl's favourite battlefield tactics.

'Quickly! Inside!'

He opened the lid and they jumped in.

The Schnurrbarts rounded the corner. The noise of their boots was muffled by the stacks of towels inside the laundry basket.

Concentrate. Don't breathe. Don't move.

Through the gaps in the wicker basket, Sheldon saw the Schnurrbarts drop into practiced attack positions and scan the maintenance area with their guns. And what weapons they were. Squat, snub-nosed, brutal looking, the guns looked about as ugly as a metallic pit bull terrier.

'What the hell *are* those things?' hissed Sheldon.

'Multiversers,' whispered The Brain.

'Multiversers?'

'I've been thinking about them ever since we saw what happened to Knut, and to the cuckoo clock. Remember how Knut was replaced by the blue chicken? And the clock by that glowing crystal pyramid? If my theory is correct— and I'm sure, as usual, that it is—a multiverser is a weapon that bounces the victim from one universe into another. Given the fact that there would be an infinite number of alternative universes, being hit by a multiverser would mean instant transportation to an unknown and potentially lethal environment. And, of course, whatever occupies the space in the alternative universe is then transported back *here*.'

'Oh, good,' whispered Sheldon. 'Because I was worrying they might be, you know, dangerous or something.'

'Quiet,' hissed The Brain. 'They're right here.'

From their hiding place, The Brain and Sheldon watched as the three Schnurrbarts began to systematically search the maintenance room. They looked like they knew what they were doing. And why wouldn't they, thought Sheldon? They were, after all, complete Captain Schnurrbarts right down to the sparkle on the toecaps of their combat boots. And if there was one thing Sheldon knew for certain about Captain Schnurrbart, it was that he was as professional as professionals come. Which meant it was only a matter of time before they'd be discovered. They were sitting ducks.

Then for a moment the Schnurrbarts disappeared from sight as they went to search a small office space off the main maintenance room.

This might be their only chance.

The Brain scanned the room for an escape route, running a practised eye across the smooth walls in search of a hatchway, a previously unseen door, anything. There was nothing. He turned his attention to the ceiling.

A narrow ridge betrayed the edge of a ceiling tile about a metre square. The Brain nodded upwards. 'If we can get into the roof space we might be able to slip away. These suspended ceilings should take our weight.'

Sheldon nodded. It was something of a plan. They moved to a position directly under the loose tile. It was tantalisingly out of reach.

Sheldon dropped onto all fours. 'Use my back as a step,' he hissed. 'Quick!'

The Schnurrbarts were backing out of the office just as The Brain stepped onto Sheldon. 'My back, I said!' mumbled Sheldon. 'Not my flaming neck!'

'Apologies, old boy,' murmured The Brain as he levered the tile free and hoisted himself into the roof space. He turned and reached a hand towards Sheldon. 'I'll pull you up.'

Sheldon took The Brain's hand just as the first of the Schnurrbarts turned and spotted them.

'Quickly!' urged The Brain and heaved Sheldon towards the opening.

Too late.

A blip of light shot from the squat nose of a multiverser and slammed into Sheldon. For a micro-second he looked despairingly into The Brain's eyes. Then he disappeared. A soggy lump of greenish goo sat in The Brain's hand.

The Brain cursed, flung the goo to the floor and, bent almost double, raced away through the roof space into the darkness.

Sheldon blinked his eyes open and in a horrifying flash he remembered what had happened. He'd been shot!

Again.

This was becoming something of a habit. A habit he'd prefer to change. If he ever got the chance, that is. What had The Brain said about the multiversers? One shot and you were transported into an alternative universe?

He looked around, expecting to be on some distant alien planet surrounded by flesh-eating robots, or something along those lines. Knowing his luck, that would be exactly the kind of alternative universe he'd end up in. On the other hand, he supposed, brightening for a moment, he could end up in some sort of paradise universe. All palm trees and pretty girls serving him delicious drinks while he lay in a hammock.

As it turned out, it was neither.

25

At first, Sheldon thought that nothing much had happened. He still appeared to be in LURV. He was standing on the mezzanine level above what looked very like the canteen.

Sheldon looked up. The Brain had disappeared. So had the ceiling. Or, to be strictly accurate, the ceiling Sheldon now found himself looking at was not the same ceiling as the one he'd been trying to climb into. Instead, it seemed to be constructed of something that reminded Sheldon of . . . coral. There was something else different, too; something odd about the air. Sheldon's movements seemed slower, the atmosphere thicker.

As he was puzzling over this, a dark shape drifted into view about a metre off the floor. It was a large grey reef shark wearing a lab coat and carrying a clipboard under a fin. Paralysed, Sheldon watched it slide past.

'Top o' the mornin',' said the shark conversationally and winked. 'No rest for the wicked, eh?'

The shark spoke in a distinct Irish accent. Gaping, Sheldon watched the shark swim down the stairs and into the main part of the canteen.

Swim.

The shark was swimming.

With a sickening jolt Sheldon realised that he was underwater. Underwater!

That wasn't good. He tried to take a breath, choked and clawed frantically at his throat. He was drowning!

Two lobsters, one large, one small, both wearing T-shirts and baseball caps, scuttled past as Sheldon flailed his arms. They looked at him curiously.

'Dad,' said the smaller one, 'what's that funny looking fish doing?'

The larger lobster stopped and looked closer at Sheldon, whose complexion was beginning to resemble that of the lobsters themselves.

'Can I help you, feller?' asked the lobster in a worried voice. 'Something stuck in your throat? I can get someone to do the Heimlich manoeuvre, if you like. I'd do it but ...' He held his claws up and shrugged.

'*Can't. Breathe,*' sputtered Sheldon. '*Drow. Ning.*'

'That sure *is* one funny-looking fish, Dad,' said the small lobster. 'Kinda ugly too.'

'Quiet, Leroy,' said the large lobster. 'This feller needs some help.'

He scuttled to the edge of the upper deck and shouted in the direction of the canteen below. 'Hey! Someone help! We got a weird-looking fish up here with something in his throat! We need someone with arms!'

There was a flurry of activity and a variety of fishy creatures swam up the stairs. A big, smartly-dressed octopus swam to the front.

'Move back, please,' it said. 'I'm a doctor.'

'Hey!' said Leroy, 'A Doctorpus! Get it?'

'Best hurry up, doc,' said the large lobster. 'He looks like he's in trouble.'

'Careful,' said Leroy. 'He might be dangerous!'

The octopus grabbed hold of Sheldon with three tentacles and jerked his stomach violently.

'Come on, fish!' the octopus grunted. 'Breathe!'

Sheldon coughed and drew in a huge lungful of water.

'That's the ticket!' said the octopus, relaxing his hold. 'Just let it come. Get those gills working!'

Sheldon sank to the floor. It was hopeless. He was never going to get out of this watery universe alive. He sucked in some more water. He might as well get it over with.

The other creatures looked at him, concerned. A few minutes passed. The crowd of onlookers began to think that the weird-looking fish on the floor wasn't quite as interesting as they'd hoped. A few began to shuffle impatiently and one or two drifted away.

'You OK?' said the large lobster looking at an expensive watch on his claw. 'Just that we gotta catch the tour group.'

'Come on, Dad,' said Leroy. 'I wanna see the celerator.'

With a shrug, the large lobster scuttled off with his son.

Drowning was taking longer than Sheldon had imagined. After several minutes he realised that he was breathing quite happily. He floated to his feet and took a few experimental snorts through his nose. Water streamed in, and then back out again as normal as 'real' breathing.

'Good work!' said the octopus, slapping him on the back. 'Glad to see you back on your, um . . . tails. Mustn't stop. Got a busy day.'

He picked up his briefcase and undulated back down the staircase. 'You sure you're OK?' he said as he slid from view.

Sheldon nodded. He was as OK as he was ever going to be. He swam in the direction the octopus had taken. He wasn't looking forward to life as a fish.

26

Captain Schnurrbart paced backwards and forwards across the rubberised floor of the SSSU control room and stroked his moustache thoughtfully. 'Status report?' He looked down at the SSSU dispatcher seated at the main computer.

The man adjusted his headset and tapped out a few commands on the keyboard. 'Nothing, sir. Nothing yet. The chopper reports no unusual surface activity. And no sign from Urtl that anything's wrong.'

Captain Schnurrbart shook his head. 'I don't like it. I don't like it one little bit, and I'm liking it less and less with every minute that passes. Urtl should have made *some* sort of progress report by now.'

The dispatcher looked up at his commanding officer. 'I could send her a signal, sir. On the quiet. Just to get her to contact us.'

Captain Schnurrbart nodded. He didn't, as a rule, contact agents when they were working undercover. If the communication happened while they were in a ticklish situation it could expose them to all kinds of dangers. But something about the silence from LURV was setting off all sorts of alarm bells. As a committed man of science, Schnurrbart didn't believe in anything he couldn't measure or observe. But as a lawman he sometimes got a tickle in his moustache when something was wrong. And right now his moustache tickled more than if he'd had a ferret covered in itching powder dancing on his upper lip. If contacting Urtl blew her cover then so be it: he'd deal with the bleatings from the high-ups at LURV.

'Do it,' he said.

The dispatcher pressed a few keys and there was a soft crackle of static as the computer sent a signal directly to Miss Urtl's earpiece.

'Put it on speaker,' said Captain Schnurrbart.

The dispatcher flicked a switch and Urtl's voice came through, low and calm.

'Yes?' she said, wasting no words on chit chat. Training reinforced the need for secrecy at all times, and Urtl was one of SSSU's most thorough agents.

'It's Schnurrbart,' said the Captain into the mike. His tone was sharp. 'Status report please.'

Urtl should have known better. Especially with members of his family on the mission. If she didn't have a decent excuse for not checking in before now, she'd be undercover at that toxic sewage plant they were investigating in Kazakhstan faster than she could say 'career over'.

There was a pause from Urtl. 'Status report?' She sounded puzzled.

'Yes, Urtl!' snapped Captain Schnurrbart, his irritation growing by the second. 'I need an immediate status report.'

'Another one?' said Urtl through the static.

Captain Schnurrbart shot a questioning glance at the dispatcher who shook his head. 'What the hell do you mean, "another one"?' he asked. 'We haven't had anything through the system here!'

Urtl spoke again. 'I haven't sent anything via radio sir.'

This was getting ridiculous. Captain Schnurrbart felt his temper rise. 'Then how in God's name have you given me a status report?'

There was silence from Urtl.

'Urtl! Answer please! How did you send the last report?'

'I didn't send it sir,' said Urtl in a slow, even voice. 'I gave it directly to you, face-to-face in the cafeteria here at LURV not two minutes ago. Don't you remember?'

Captain Schnurrbart stood up from the microphone as though it was contagious. The dispatcher and the rest of the SSSU control room team looked at each other.

'Sir?' Urtl's voice came through the control room speakers. 'Awaiting instructions.'

Captain Schnurrbart bent once more to speak. Before he could, a loud blast of noise came through from Urtl's radio. There were shouts, screams, bangs, a grunt from Urtl and then silence.

'URTL!' yelled Captain Schnurrbart. 'Status report!'

The dispatcher shook his head and turned to Captain Schnurrbart. 'She's gone, sir. Radio contact lost.'

Schnurrbart banged his hand down on the desktop. First Knut, now Urtl. He was *not* going to lose another agent on this thing! 'Get a squad organised, Frimmel,' he said in a determined voice. 'Twenty agents, fully armed and ready to go. Chopper two takes off in three minutes from the roof. We're going in.'

27

Mr Smit, the LURV tour guide, did a quick mental recap and had to admit the tour was not going well. He'd be lucky to come out of this with his job.

Three of the schoolchildren had vanished so far, and it wasn't even lunchtime. On the other hand, the kids who had slipped away from the tour group had looked like troublemakers. That kid with the big head and the glasses, and his two little friends. Smit wasn't even a tiny bit sorry to see those particular specimens disappear.

He was not worried that they would come to any harm. Security at LURV was tight and it was only a matter of time before all of them were found and returned to the tour. Smit would make sure that the teachers got a piece of his mind before the day was out. The woman teacher, Miss Urtl, had slipped out into the corridor. He shot a withering glance in the direction of Herr Gustaffson who was sitting to one side looking like he'd rather be anywhere else than on a school trip.

Smit called an early lunch to stall the tour group in the LURV cafeteria, where he could keep a watchful eye on the rest of the little troublemakers. At least that way the tour would be over sooner. There was something about today's group that rubbed Smit up the wrong way. Too cocky by half, he'd have said, if anyone had asked.

Which they hadn't.

He turned his attention back to his cheese sandwich. The woman had given him the wrong cheese. He'd specifically asked for Swiss cheese but, after a brief inspection of the contents, Smit had established that his cheese was entirely free of holes.

I *like* the holes, he thought, before taking a weary bite. It was definitely one of those days when he'd have been better off back checking readings in the lab.

Suddenly, there was a commotion in the hall outside.

Smit looked up as the double doors to the cafeteria burst open and Miss Urtl hurtled into the nearest table, sending plates, salt shakers and food skittling across the tiles. She was grappling furiously with a large man sporting a black moustache. As the two rolled across the canteen floor, Miss Urtl cracked her head on a chair before twisting and looking at her attacker.

'Captain Schnurrbart!' yelled Miss Urtl. 'What's got into you? Don't make me hurt you!'

Captain Schnurrbart didn't answer. Instead he jabbed his right hand at the carotid artery in Miss Urtl's neck. A Mongolian death strike.

Miss Urtl dodged the blow and jabbed a thumb right into Schnurrbart's eye.

He yelled and kicked her hard, karate style, in the kidneys.

'*Oooof!*' The breath left Miss Urtl.

It was the sort of blow that would have stopped a lesser woman in her tracks. Frankly, thought Smit, that kick would have stopped a hippo dead. But Miss Urtl was made of sterner stuff than most people, not to mention most hippos. Ignoring the searing pain in her side, she back-flipped fluidly into an upright fighting stance and advanced on the scowling Captain Schnurrbart. The two circled each other warily, making small forward and backward motions, watching for an opportunity to strike.

'Miss Urtl! Captain Schnurrbart!' cried Herr Gustaffson in a shocked voice. 'What on earth do you think you are doing?'

Urtl and Schnurrbart ignored him. There was no room for distraction. The combatants eyed each other warily.

A noise echoed from the corridor; the clang of boots on concrete. Schnurrbart glanced back at the doors. It was all the space Urtl needed. She flicked her cardigan off in one swift movement and cracked it like a whip. One of the specially weighted stone buttons connected sharply with Schnurrbart's temple and he fell like a tasered ox. Her skirts whirling, Miss Urtl leapt forward and drew back her hand in a death blow stance she had learnt from a Tibetan monk.

Before she could deliver the fatal strike, the doors flew open once more and the rest of the Schnurrbarts poured in. Miss Urtl sprang upright and turned to the stunned tour group.

'Run!' she yelled. 'Now!'

Then a blip of light shot from a multiverser and she was gone, replaced by an object that looked a little like a toilet except that it was two metres tall. A thin, greenish-coloured creature, half-man, half-biscuit, sat on top of it reading what might have been a newspaper. He looked around at the mayhem in the cafeteria and gave a squeak of panic.

Smit sat stunned as children scattered in every direction around him. Herr Gustaffson, to his eternal credit, did his best to stop the Schnurrbarts. It was useless. Before he could get close enough to do anything, he was hit by a blast from a multiverser and sent directly to a universe where he was greeted as a god by worshipping multitudes. In his place a column of brightly coloured spiders appeared, each the size of a dinner plate, and scuttled off into the kitchens where they caused a cook to faint into a batch of mayonnaise.

Back in the cafeteria, the Schnurrbarts were advancing ruthlessly across the room, picking off the SSSU tour group one by one.

Blap!

Linder Bleck was catapulted into a parallel universe where apes ran the planet. A surprised green monkey in a tuxedo appeared in her place and ran away screeching.

Blap!

Jan Futtnick copped a blast on his shoulder and was flung straight into a universe that believed in human sacrifice. Jan, most unfortunately for him, replaced the would-be victim who, after a moment of absolute surprise, gave a whoop of delight and danced away, his arms raised in celebration.

Blap!

Franck and Erich, the twins, were bounced directly into a universe of all powerful women who treated men and boys as slaves. A chair made of dried cow dung appeared in their place and toppled over, breaking into pieces.

Blap! Blap! Blap!

The remaining members of the SSSU tour group were multiversed into alternate universes and the cafeteria rapidly began to fill with an incredible assortment of objects, creatures and parts of odd-looking buildings. A vibrating mass of transparent yellow jelly that had appeared in place of a student, seized a nearby Schnurrbart and began to eat him. He could be clearly seen inside the yellow creature gesturing frantically to be rescued. The two panthers that had chased The Brain and Sheldon earlier, appeared at the door, took one disgusted look and sloped away. A metallic-looking snake creature that had replaced Mrs Mongrove, the cafeteria manager, was coiling itself around an air-conditioning duct and singing what sounded like a love song in French.

Smit had not moved a centimetre. He sat at his table and watched the chaos unfold, a half-eaten cheese sandwich raised to his still-open mouth. One of the Schnurrbarts aimed a snub-nosed multiverser at him and pulled the trigger.

Smit was enough of a scientist to have guessed by now just what the multiversers were doing. The evidence was there for an informed eye to see. He shut his eyes and hoped he wouldn't end up anywhere too horrible. The blast from the multiverser hit him full on and he experienced a momentary feeling of nausea before opening his eyes.

'Look, Dad!' said a high-pitched voice. 'It's another one of those funny-looking fish!'

Smit looked down to see two lobsters, one large, one small, looking up at him in astonishment. He took a breath to ask them where he was and realised he was underwater. He clutched at his throat and thrashed around.

'Holy moley!' said the large lobster. 'Here we go again! Son, fetch that doctorpus, will you?'

28

If you look up the word 'coincidence' on the internet you will find the following: 'co-in-ci-dence (*koh-in-si-duhns*). Noun. A striking occurrence of two or more events at one time apparently by mere chance.'

If you type in the words 'unbelievable, outrageous, mind-boggling coincidence' you may find it defined as what happened at the cafeteria when Smit was bounced into the fishy universe that Sheldon had recently been transported into. If the multiverse contains an infinite number of universes, then the chances of Sheldon being whisked out of the universe he had found himself in, and discovering that he had been returned to *the exact universe he had left*, would be so astronomical as to be beyond belief.

Yet that is precisely what happened.

Coughing furiously, Sheldon appeared in the cafeteria in place of the unfortunate Smit. His clothes drenched, he spluttered and hawked up a surprisingly large amount of water onto the floor. In front of him, the Schnurrbart who had shot Smit with the multiverser stopped dead in his tracks. He raised the gun again and then lowered it again, uncertain of what to do. Sheldon's reappearance did not fit into any of the Schnurrbarts' battle tactics. As Sheldon waited to be hit by another blip from the multiverser, he had no way of knowing that the Schnurrbart was thinking back to the briefing they'd had before being handed the multiversers.

The multiversers, they had been told, were extremely powerful weapons and were not to be taken lightly. Misuse could lead to some very strange things happening. Quite what those strange things were, and exactly how shooting Sheldon once again with the multiverser would lead to those effects, the Schnurrbart couldn't say. Still, it would not do to cross the Chief on this one. The risk, however minimal, was still too much. The Schnurrbart slung his multiverser across his back and decided to deal with Sheldon by more conventional means.

Sheldon had not sat passively while the Schnurrbart came to this decision. He had formed a plan. A plan that involved him palming a squeezable economy-size bottle of tomato sauce. As the Schnurrbart advanced, his hands outstretched, Sheldon whipped out the sauce, aimed it dead at the Schnurrbart and squeezed. Hard.

A jet of vinegary ketchup shot directly into the Schnurrbart's eyes. With a howl of anguish he clutched his hands to his face and fell to his knees.

Another Schnurrbart nearby saw the tomato sauce and jumped to the wrong conclusion. '*Medic!*' he screamed into his shoulder radio. 'Man down! Medic to the cafeteria, I repeat, medic to the cafeteria! Major trauma! I repeat, major trauma!'

Sheldon slipped on the wet floor, recovered, and scrambled over the cafeteria counter into the kitchen area. He skirted a couple of monstrous spiders that had pinned a maintenance worker to the floor and bolted for the back exit, his mind fixed on one thing and one thing only.

Where was Helga?

But to find Helga, he needed to find The Brain. The Brain would sort everything out.

Wouldn't he?

29

At that very moment The Brain was sitting at a computer console in the control room. Some of the creatures and objects that had replaced those unfortunate enough to have been hit by the multiversers had wandered in, lending it the air of a very strange art exhibit, or a particularly freaky zoo. A large jungle-like plant-creature was showing an interest in Professor Weiss and the rest of the shrunken control room crew, mistaking them for after dinner snacks popular in its home universe. A mermaid sat on a computer and began to sing a sad song.

The Brain tried to ignore the chaos.

'Come on, Pandora,' he murmured, as he bent over the computer interface. 'Show me what you've been up to, you naughty girl.'

His bony white fingers flew across the keys like octopus tap dancers as he gazed intently at the large flat-screen monitor. Ranks of numbers scrolled downwards. Information flowed from and to The Brain as he hooked himself into the largest and most powerful computer on the planet. To a casual observer, The Brain would have appeared as icily cool as ever. Only a faint tic in the corner of his left eye betrayed the enormous tension he was under.

On the screen the scale of the disaster that had been unleashed at LURV began to take shape.

He tapped furiously, stopping now and then to consider something or alter a keystroke. Around him, distantly, he could hear the mayhem unfolding. Yet, *tap, tap, tap*, he continued, his concentration absolute.

And then it was all there. In glowing electronic digits onscreen. Everything laid out in neat rows of binary code translated into numbers, words, time, all pointing to one thing: the mastermind who was behind the events at LURV.

'Of course,' he whispered. 'Who else?'

And with this discovery, Theophilus Nero Hercule Sherlock Wimsey Father Brown Marlowe Spade Christie Edgar Allen Brain knew it was down to him to save LURV, Switzerland—and, quite possibly, the universe—from descending into complete and utter silliness.

He just wished he knew how.

Sheldon ran blindly from room to room looking for The Brain. Door after door was flung open to reveal creatures and parts of landscapes from other universes. But of Theo there was no sign. Several times, Sheldon had only just managed to duck out of the way of a group of Schnurrbarts rampaging through the complex, multiversers at the ready. Sheldon gritted his teeth. After his experience in the fish universe, there was no way he was going to let one of those goons send him anywhere like that again. He could still taste the brine in his mouth and his damp clothes chafed something rotten.

He paused in the gloom of a cloakroom, sat down on a bench below a rack of coats and tried to think clearly. There must be something he could do. He had to find a way to contact the real Captain Schnurrbart and tip him off about what was happening.

The difficulty was, how was he going to call Captain Schnurrbart? He didn't have one of those spiffy 'work any-where' radios that the SSSU officers had. He could call him on the phone, he supposed. If he could find one that worked. And if he could remember the phone number of SSSU headquarters.

Sheldon looked around the cloak room. He thought he had heard the theme tune from a popular cartoon show. It was coming from one of the coats.

A mobile phone.

He moved along the line of coats until he found the right one. He patted the pockets and lifted out a slim, silver mobile. He snapped it open.

'Ernst?' said a voice. '*Ist das Sie? Wann sind Sie Haupt?*'

'Sorry,' said Sheldon. '*Ich spreche nicht Deutsches.*'

He pressed the 'end call' button and tried to remember the SSSU number. Then it came to him in a flash. Bold eggs! He recalled how the Captain had explained how to remember the number.

'If you type 5663 0708 in on a calculator and hold it upside down it spells 'BOLD EGGS'. 5663 0708. Bold eggs, simple.'

Sheldon tapped out the number and clamped the phone to his ear. It rang. And rang again. On the third ring someone answered.

'Yes?'

'Captain Schnurrbart,' hissed Sheldon. 'I need to speak urgently to Captain Schnurrbart! Code black!'

There was a click on the line and for a moment Sheldon thought whoever had answered had hung up. Then a crackle of static and the familiar voice of Captain Schnurrbart came through. Wherever he was, it was somewhere noisy.

'Schnurrbart,' he said crisply. 'Who is this?'

Sheldon could have wept with relief. 'It's me Captain: Sheldon. You have to get here quick. Everything's happening and the fa . . .'

Captain Schnurrbart cut in.

'Stop babbling, Sheldon! I need you to be calm. We're on our way, ETA three minutes. Now, where should we head for once we get to LURV?'

Sheldon thought for a second. Where was Helga? Where was The Brain? Where should the SSSU target when they arrived? LURV was enormous. It could take them hours to find the Schnurrbarts and by then it could be too late. He could only hope that Helga was still Helga and hadn't been multiversed somewhere horrible.

And then in a flash it came to him where The Brain would be. Whatever was happening, it had something to do with Pandora.

'The main control room,' said Sheldon. 'Head for the main control room!'

Captain Schnurrbart didn't reply. With a fizz of static the line went dead.

Sheldon cursed and re-dialled. Nothing. He tried three more times before he noticed the dead battery signal on the mobile phone. He had no way of knowing if the Captain had heard his last message.

He just had to hope.

Sheldon cautiously opened the cloakroom door and stuck his nose out. He couldn't see anything with his nose, so he stuck an eye out too. The corridor was empty apart from a flame-coloured chicken with five legs that was strolling round the nearest corner, whistling happily. Sheldon ignored the chicken. Most of the recent arrivals from alternate universes seemed so shocked by their sudden change in circumstances that they were pretty harmless. The main thing was that the corridor showed no sign of a Schnurrbart goon squad.

Sheldon stepped out and set off towards the control room.

He hadn't taken more than fifty paces when he sensed someone coming round the corner. With a rising sense of panic he looked around for a hiding place and saw nothing. Not a cupboard, a hatchway, a laundry basket. He was too far from the last corner to run back. Whatever was coming would be there before he could make it. If this was the Schnurrbarts then Sheldon decided he'd rather go down fighting in a glorious hail of multiverser blips.

He set his face into a mask of determination and roared round the corner, a bloodthirsty scream on his lips. He'd achieved full running speed when ran slap into Helga. Together they rolled across the floor and came to rest against a wall.

'We have to stop meeting like this,' said Helga, rubbing her forehead. 'First in the Furcht, and now here! Don't you believe in just saying "hi"?'

'I—I,' Sheldon stammered.

Helga put her arms round him and hugged him tightly. 'I thought you'd been eaten!' she said.

'No,' Sheldon said. 'We didn't, they couldn't ... I mean, oh I don't know what I mean!' With Helga's arms around him he found that logical thought was impossible.

She let go and stood up. 'The important thing is that you're OK! I overheard the man in charge of the whole thing talking and whatever they're doing, they're going to do it now,' she said. 'And it's down to us to stop them and find my father.'

'I think it may already be too late,' said Sheldon.

In a jumbled rush of words he poured out everything that had happened to him: the fish universe, the Schnurrbarts, his own re-appearance back in LURV.

He didn't mention he'd eaten her father. It seemed like the wrong time to bring up a thing like that. Not that Sheldon could ever imagine there being a good time.

'But you look great!' babbled Sheldon. 'That is, I mean, you look in good shape. No, not that! Oh, I mean, yes you are in good shape, of course you are, you look good. I mean, you always look great but I thought what with everything that's been happening here and all those weird multiversers and the octopus and the ...'

'Sheldon,' Helga said calmly.

'Yes?'

'You're babbling. I need you, *we* need you to stop babbling. Now.'

'Oh, yes. Right-oh. Of course. No babbling. I completely understand. I won't babble anymore. I absolutely promise not to do any more babbli—'

Helga shook him. 'You're doing it again.'

Sheldon sucked in a deep breath and remained silent.

'All calm?' said Helga.

Sheldon nodded meekly.

'Good. Now we can get somewhere. The first thing to do is to find The Brain.'

'I think,' said Sheldon cautiously, 'that he might be in the control centre.'

'You're sure?'

'Well no, not really,' said Sheldon uncertainly. 'It's just an idea . . .'

'And a good one, too. Of course that is where we will find The Brain. Where else would he be? We have to get there right away.'

Sheldon nodded. As plans went, it sounded like a good idea but it was, he had to admit, a little sketchy on exactly *how* they were going to stop the Schnurrbarts and their mysterious Chief. He decided not to mention his concerns to Helga. He didn't want her to think he was babbling again.

Helga took Sheldon's hand and pulled him towards a nearby lift. She pressed the button and the lift doors slid open. They stepped inside and the doors closed. As Helga busied herself with the control panel, Sheldon fidgeted behind her. There was something he'd been meaning to tell Helga ever since he'd set eyes on her that snowy night when she'd first arrived. Basically, that she was the most beautiful creature he'd ever seen. And now he might only get this short lift ride to let her know her hair was like the finest spun silk and her eyes were limpid pools of emerald.

'H-Helga,' he stammered.

'Mm?' said Helga, still intent on the lift buttons.

'There's something I've been meaning to, um, say to you. That is, if you don't mind, I wanted to say that your eyes . . .'

'Yes?' said Helga, turning around. 'What about my eyes?'

Sheldon stared at his feet, beetroot with embarrassment, but determined to see it through. 'Your eyes,' he said. 'They, they . . .'

Sheldon took a deep breath, raised his gaze from his shoes and looked straight at Helga. 'Your eyes are,' he began. He stopped mid-sentence and blinked. Oh, what was the use? This girl stuff was like learning Swahili.

Enough talking. This was maybe his last chance before the universe exploded, or shrank, or filled with inflatable dinosaurs, or whatever weird fate was in store for it from the evil Schnurrbarts and the Chief. Now or never.

Sheldon closed his eyes, leaned forward and kissed Helga full on the mouth.

The lift doors slid open and a distinctive voice echoed through the compartment.

'Gorblimey, ain't that sweet! Look gents, it's true LURV!'

There in the doorway, a Schnurrbart on either side of him, stood Stokes the two-headed butler.

The Chief.

30

'Sheldon? Sheldon? Can you hear me, Sheldon?'

Captain Schnurrbart swore under his breath and pressed a button on his helmet microphone. 'Can you get me that line back, Officer Hefferning?' he said. 'He just cut out.'

'Negative, Captain, sorry,' said Hefferning, his voice thick with static. 'The line's out. No signal.'

'Keep trying,' said Captain Schnurrbart. 'If you get him online again patch it through to me. At least we know he's alive. And where to head for. The boy's done well.'

He picked up a pair of high-powered binoculars and turned his attention back to LURV.

The SSSU chopper banked steeply around the side of the Ulterschorn, the Alpine peak that towered above the LURV complex, as Captain Schnurrbart scanned the site.

'Nothing moving,' he muttered into his helmet microphone. His second-in-command looked at him and raised his eyebrows.

'Exactly, Frimmel,' said the Captain. '*Why* isn't there anything moving? You'd expect delivery trucks, maintenance staff, security. Someone, something, should be visible.' Schnurrbart pointed to a car park to one side of the main entrance. 'Put her down right there.'

The pilot nodded and the craft dipped towards LURV.

Captain Schnurrbart shifted round in his seat and

looked back at the twin ranks of SSSU agents sitting silently in the main body of the Chinook.

'Full alert status, gentlemen,' he said quietly. 'No need to remind you that this is a dangerous operation. We don't want to lose another agent. And remember; there's a school party in there.'

The agents nodded. Schnurrbart checked his gear and waited for the chopper to touch down. He had to use all his self-control not to jump clear of the helicopter before it landed, such was his desire to get on with the job, to rescue Sheldon and Theo, to fix this awful mess. He should never have agreed to send the children in; he could see that now.

The wheels of the helicopter bumped softly onto the concrete and Captain Schnurrbart dropped instantly out of the door and hit the ground running, his breath streaming out in the cold mountain air. Behind him, the rest of the squad exited through the Chinook's large cargo door and sprinted for the main entrance. The Chinook flew low in front of them, masking them from possible attack, before sweeping skywards as they reached the front doors. The squad split into three sections. With four men either side of the double doors, the rest formed into a flying wedge formation, Schnurrbart at the front. The SSSU burst into LURV in a clatter of boots on tile.

The lobby was deserted, silent. Two SSSU agents cautiously approached the desk and checked behind it. A glowing lump of pink jelly sat on the stool where the LURV receptionist usually sat. Officer Frimmel poked the jelly with the tip of his gun and it dissolved into dust. Frimmel and Pathfinder checked the rest of the reception area and looked up at the three banks of security monitors.

'You need to see this, sir,' said Frimmel.

Captain Schnurrbart nodded and walked around to the operational side of the lobby reception desk. The monitors showed images of most parts of the LURV complex. At first glance all appeared calm. Shots of bland corridors and nondescript office spaces filled the screens. Schnurrbart had almost turned away from the screens when a sudden movement caught his eye.

'There!' he barked and pointed.

He and Frimmel watched, astonished, as two black panthers strolled past the camera. Schnurrbart rubbed his eyes and looked at Frimmel. On another monitor twelve Amazonian warriors holding lethal-looking spears and carrying long decorated shields jogged past in tight formation.

'What the—' said Schnurrbart under his breath.

Frimmel nudged his commanding officer and pointed to a monitor showing a view of a room filled with computers and electronic equipment. A man moved slowly through the desks, his snub-nosed weapon raised to shoulder height as he looked for something. As he passed directly in front of the security camera he turned his face briefly and it caught the light. Frimmel gasped. The man on screen was clearly Captain Schnurrbart. Beside him, the real Schnurrbart gasped, too.

'*Mon Dieu!*' whispered Frimmel, who looked as though he'd seen a ghost. He crossed himself automatically and looked wide-eyed at the real Captain Schnurrbart as if expecting him to vanish at any moment.

'Snap out of it, Frimmel,' said Captain Schnurrbart impatiently. 'It's a doppelganger, a mirage, some sort of holographic trickery, that's all!'

He turned away from the screens, more shaken than he allowed his men to see.

What was going on down here?

31

The Brain sat back, his arms folded, and thought about the problem facing him. If he was correct about the data he'd got from Pandora—and he had no doubt that he was, as usual, absolutely right—then he and everyone else didn't have too long left before everything went Very Silly Indeed.

Unless The Brain did something about it. And soon.

The big question, the one that kept him sitting in front of the console, was what, exactly?

And then he had an idea.

It was a ridiculous, nonsensical idea. One that had absolutely no right to work at all. Yet it did have one outstanding feature: it was the only idea The Brain had.

It would have to do.

He scooted his chair back to the keyboard and tapped into Pandora once more.

'Come along, old girl,' he murmured. 'Let's see if we can sort this little spot of bother out, shall we?'

His fingers hummed across the keys. In another age, another place, people would have paid good money to watch a young Mozart or Michelangelo at work and marvel at the skill, the artistry. It was at that same level that The Brain's fingers now tapped. He played Pandora like others played a concert piano. Conscious that he was sitting at the centre of the globe's most powerful (and, if he was right, most dangerous) computer, The Brain felt his own astonishing mental abilities respond to the challenge facing him. The screen glowed green and blue in front of him as binary code flowed in a symphony of data. It was poetry. It was art. It was almost, almost there—

The doors to the control room burst open behind The Brain. He did not bother to look up from his mission. 'Ah, Stokes,' he said quietly. 'Please take a seat. Forgive me for not getting up. This may take me a few more moments.'

If Stokes was surprised The Brain knew it was him, he didn't show it. 'Move away from the computer,' said one of his heads.

'Before I get someone to move you,' said the other.

The Brain tapped a final 'return' key and pushed himself away from the keyboard. He swivelled slowly and faced the butler. The man was still in the familiar butler suit, but he looked different, more dangerous.

'Could you get me a cup of tea, please?' asked The Brain. 'Earl Grey, lemon, no sugar.'

'Very funny,' said one of Stokes's heads. 'You 'ear that, Stokes? The young gent seems to be a bit of a joker.'

'Is that right, Stokes?' said the other head. 'Then I 'ope he likes the punch line.'

Number One stood behind Stokes, Sheldon's limp body slung casually over his shoulder. In his other hand he was holding Helga in a vice-like grip. For a fraction of a second a tremor of rage passed across The Brain's normally calm face.

'Don't worry,' said Stokes's left head. 'Yer little friend fainted when he realised my true colours, so to speak. He's alive, or at least I fink he is. It's so 'ard to tell with these lower life forms, don't you find?'

'I trust you're not including me on any list that includes you?' The Brain's tone matched that of Stokes for coldness. He peered at him through his glasses. The lights winked off his lenses and gave him an air of remoteness. 'It took longer than I expected for you to reveal yourself,' he added. 'Now, if you don't mind, would you be so good as to let go of my friend? He will have suffered enough without waking up to find himself in that undignified position.'

Stokes made a gesture to Number One who casually tossed Sheldon onto the floor, where he lay crumpled at The Brain's feet. After a second or two, Sheldon groaned and sat up slowly, rubbing his head.

'Helga!' he said and started to rise to his feet.

The Brain reached out and held his shoulder.

'Pray remain still, old bean,' he said. 'You've had a bit of a shock and too much movement may prove harmful.'

'I'm fine, Sheldon,' said Helga. 'Do what The Brain says.'

Sheldon glared at Stokes.

'But, but ... you're a butler! Butlers don't take over top-secret science places! Do they?'

Stokes chuckled. 'In this case, my son,' he said, 'it's safe to say that the butler did it.'

'What about Weiss and all the other people you've multi-versed?' said The Brain.

'Weiss was a useful tool, nothing else,' Stokes replied. 'Although more fond of cakes than he should have been, and far too prone to blabbing. The idiot thought I was a plaything, an amusement. A butler, I ask yer! Don't forget, *he* multiversed *me* first. I never asked him to bring me here! I played along for a while once I saw the possibilities. He's of no consequence.'

The Brain's voice was steely. 'And the others? Are they also "of no consequence"?'

Stokes nodded one of his heads. 'Precisely. Mere pawns in my cunning plan. Collateral damage.'

The Brain placed his pipe between his teeth, unlit as always. 'I blame myself,' he said. 'I should have spotted you were two-faced sooner.'

Sheldon raised a hand. 'Um, can I ask a question?'

'This isn't school, Sheldon,' said The Brain.

Sheldon looked from The Brain to Stokes and then at the Schnurrbart. 'What, exactly, is going on?'

'That's a very good question,' said Helga. 'What *is* going on?'

The Brain thrust a hand towards Stokes. 'As you have heard, it turns out that Stokes is far more dangerous than the foolish Professor Weiss could ever imagine. I warned Weiss that opening the multiverse was risky. Stokes here is proof of that. There's no way of stopping dangerous individuals like him coming through. I mean, look at him: he's nuttier than a squirrel's penthouse.'

'Pah!' snapped Stokes. 'I am a genius!'

'Well, they do say that the line between genius and madness is sometimes on the thinnish side, don't they? Unfortunately, in your case it's thinner than air and you're most definitely on the fruitcake side of the deal.'

'This is all very interesting,' said Stokes's other head, 'but I have things to do.'

Helga, who had been struggling in Number One's grip for the last couple of minutes, finally lost patience. 'Hey!' she shouted. 'Have you all forgotten about me? This *did* all start out with a search for my father, remember?'

'Your father?' Stokes looked puzzled. 'Who is he? Oh, the truck driver? Well, frankly, my dear, I don't give a damn. He must still be in that truck, I suppose. The fool couldn't even obey simple instructions! You may be better off wivout 'im.'

Helga scowled. 'If you've harmed my father,' she hissed. 'I'll—'

'You'll what, exactly?' said Stokes. 'You're completely powerless! Don't you realise that you are in the presence of the leader of a new universal order? In my universe, in my world, before that toe-rag Weiss zapped me here, I was a ruler, an Emperor, a warrior! I ruled with an iron fist and my word was law! Law! Instead of mewling about your idiotic father, you should be kneeling before me, you miserable specs of filth! I—'

'Yes, yes,' said The Brain, 'we get it Stokes—bow down, worship the all-powerful etcetera etcetera—but before you start celebrating too much, I must tell you that you don't have much time left before I put a stop to your little game.'

Stokes blinked all four eyes. Then he roared with laughter. 'You? You dare to threaten me, you maggot? I've 'ad enough of your nonsense. Get them out of my way! It's time to open up the floodgates.'

Number One moved forward and dragged The Brain and Sheldon away from the computer screen.

Stokes bent impatiently over the keyboard and tapped a number of commands. 'Excellent,' he purred. 'The time is almost upon us. There's nothing you can do now. In a few minutes the old order will cease to exist and a universe of chaos, of anarchy, will spring up in its place! One with me at the controls, natch!'

'Have you noticed, old chap,' said The Brain to Sheldon, 'that all these loopy world—or in this case universe— domination types waste so much time talking about their plans, rather than simply going ahead at doing it? Waste of time, if you ask me.'

It was clear to Sheldon that The Brain was stalling. More, he was deliberately provoking Stokes. But what for? Wasn't time on *Stokes's* side? Didn't they only have minutes left to save the universe from silliness?

Stokes turned from the computer and nodded to Number One. He'd run out of patience. 'Enough talking,' he said. 'Get rid of them.'

Number One raised his multiverser and pointed it at Sheldon.

'Goodbye, Theo,' said Sheldon, bracing himself for the flip into an unknown universe. 'Goodbye, Helga. Oh, and Helga. About your father, there's something I need to tell—'

Helga shook her head. 'You don't have to explain any-thing Sheldon,' she said. 'You did your best.'

'No,' said Sheldon, 'that's not what I meant! I—'

'Oh, for God's sake!' said Stokes, interrupting. 'Just shoot them!'

As Number One's finger curled around the trigger a figure walked into the control room and Number One hesitated.

It was one of the Schnurrbarts. He looked round the room, his face expressionless, his gun held loosely across his chest. The Brain was fairly sure that only he and Sheldon would have noticed that this Schnurrbart was not carrying a multiverser. He was carrying a regulation issue SSSU automatic rifle.

He was the real Captain Schnurrbart.

32

Stokes turned away from the new arrival with a dismissive gesture. The real Captain Schnurrbart gave The Brain the briefest of glances. With a flicker of an eyebrow he indicated a small air vent set into the wall a few paces to The Brain's left. The Brain gave no indication he'd understood, but Schnurrbart was confident he'd got the message. SSSU training was thorough and The Brain was a good student.

It was clear to Sheldon that (a) the Captain must have got his phone message and (b) if Stokes looked closely at the Captain he would soon spot he was the real deal. He needed to create a diversion.

'Hey, double-header!' he yelled. 'Before you zap me into another universe, there's something I need to tell my—'

'Your girlfriend?' said Stokes.

Sheldon nodded. 'Yes, my girlfriend. There's something she needs to know. I found her father.'

Helga stared open-mouthed at Sheldon.

'Oh, this I 'ave to hear,' chuckled Stokes. 'Pathetic though this attempt to prolong your worthless existence is!'

Sheldon exchanged glances with The Brain. Looking braver than he felt, Sheldon stepped forward to narrow the distance between himself and Helga. Number One lowered his multiverser.

Sheldon swallowed with difficulty. From just inside his

line of vision he could see the Captain slowly moving his gun into a firing position. Helga looked at Sheldon, her lovely face etched with pain.

'You see,' said Sheldon in a strangled voice. 'Here's the thing Helga, I *did* find your dad in the truck, although I didn't know it at the time. And, you see, the thing is, the thing is that—' Sheldon looked at the floor. He couldn't meet Helga's eyes. 'In the truck were some raisins that turned out not to be raisins. They were people, or at least one of them was. I was, um, hungry. I ate one of the raisins. It was your father. I ate him.'

Helga staggered as though she'd been hit with a baseball bat.

'Oh priceless!' Stokes threw back both heads and laughed. 'I'm glad I stayed for that one!'

'You *ate* him?' said Helga. 'And when were you going to tell me?'

'I only just found out,' said Sheldon miserably. 'I would have—'

'Alright, lover boy,' Stokes cut in. 'That's enough.'

He nodded to Number One who raised the multiverser just as the real Captain Schnurrbart let loose with a burst of gunfire. Behind Number One a bank of computers exploded in a shower of sparks and smoke. It was enough to knock him off balance. Number Two swung his multiverser towards the Captain and a blip of light just missed his shoulder as he somersaulted behind a rack of storage cabinets.

Taking advantage of the confusion, The Brain, Helga and Sheldon raced across the floor and crashed through the flimsy cover of the air duct. As they dropped out of sight they could hear the deafening clatter of battle. The control room was in chaos. Smoke from the smashed computers had triggered the efficient sprinkler system and water cascaded from the ceiling, soaking everything in the room in an instant. The rest of the SSSU agents poured into the control room, took up defensive positions and began firing. As the room filled with smoke and water, the gun flashes flickered and strobed everything into a jerky slow motion.

Like ghosts, the doppelganger Schnurrbarts drifted through the walls. Without missing a beat, they began firing the multiversers at the SSSU agents. It wasn't much of a contest. The SSSU bullets passed straight through the Schnurrbarts. Every time a direct hit was scored they staggered back, unhurt, but came back with the look of someone swimming against a strong current, or walking directly into a gale force wind.

On the other side, the losses were starting to rise.

One by one, the SSSU agents were picked off by blasts from the multiversers. The control room began to fill with strange creatures from other universes; a camel-like animal, a blue humanoid fifty centimetres tall, a plant that moved like a crab. The appearance of each signified the disappearance of another SSSU agent, and Captain Schnurrbart knew he was running out of both time and men. Stokes, sheltering behind a thick concrete column, glanced at the computer screen and smiled.

One more power surge from Pandora would do it.

The gateway was almost open.

*

The Brain, Sheldon and Helga fell down the air vent like stones down a well. With a bone-jarring crash, they smashed against a foil-covered air-conditioning pipe that cushioned their fall a little. Still, it took a few vital seconds for them to recover their breath. Sheldon's ribs ached and when he moved a stabbing pain made his chest feel as though he had a band of knives strapped round him.

'Think . . . rib . . . bust,' he gasped.

'Good,' said Helga. 'I hope it hurts!'

The Brain, one of the lenses of his glasses starred into a crazed spider web of cracks, patted him gently on the shoulder. 'Don't worry, old bean,' he said. 'If we don't fix this little problem in a few minutes it won't matter.'

'If . . . that's . . . supposed . . . to . . . cheer . . . me . . . up . . .' hissed Sheldon through clenched teeth.

The Brain smiled. 'Come on, let's get cracking.' He glanced at Sheldon. 'Oops, bad choice of words.'

'How *could* you?' gasped Helga.

'I didn't *know* I was eating him!' said Sheldon. 'I was . . . peckish.'

Helga directed a glare at Sheldon that would have put a hole in the side of a building. 'Peckish? You were peckish?'

'Miss Poom, Sheldon,' said The Brain. 'Time is of the essence. This discussion will have to wait.'

He kicked a wire duct cover free of its moorings and they dropped into a corridor. Sheldon winced from the pain in his ribs. The pain in his heart he could do little about.

The Brain scanned the corridor.

'We're directly below the control room,' he said.

The fact was all too obvious. The sound of gunfire and

rampaging parallel universe creatures was loud even a floor below. The Brain checked his watch.

'I make it four and a half minutes to the next power surge. And that next one is going to be big. Really big.'

He set off away from the control room, one arm around Sheldon.

'Where are we going?' asked Sheldon.

'I'm searching for something,' said The Brain. 'Something we need to stop the universe getting silly.'

Sheldon wondered what it might be. A computer override system? A quasar pulse activator? A magician? A miracle?

'What,' said Helga, 'are we looking for?'

The Brain looked at her as though she was mad. 'A vacuum cleaner, of course.'

33

'Let me get this right,' said Sheldon. 'We're going to save the universe with a vacuum cleaner?'

The Brain wasn't listening. He was deep inside a dusty maintenance cupboard picking up and then discarding various cleaning implements which he threw over his shoulder. A floor-polishing machine was pushed roughly out of the way.

'Couldn't we use that floor polisher instead?'

'There's no need for sarcasm,' said The Brain, emerging triumphantly from the cupboard clutching an ancient vacuum cleaner.

It was a heavy object, an old industrial model with a solid metal base and an upright handle. A thick, rubberised canvas bag held the dust. A long, thick, electrical flex dangled from the machine's handle. The Brain blew a cloud of dust from its old-fashioned bag.

'Miss Poom,' said The Brain. 'Would you give me a hand with this? It's rather heavy and Sheldon is incapacitated.'

'Will this get rid of that two-headed freak?' said Helga.

The Brain nodded. 'I believe so.'

'Then count me in.' She grabbed one end of the vacuum cleaner and they raced down the corridor.

The Brain and Helga manoeuvred the vacuum cleaner up a set of stairs and headed at a trot towards the control room.

Sheldon snorted in disgust, but followed as fast as the pain in his ribs allowed. Now that he had a chance to think about it, it was clear what had happened. The situation had proved too much even for The Brain. The events of the past few days had completely unhinged him. Hadn't he once said that the line between genius and madness was a thin one? Going back into that battle armed with nothing more than a vacuum cleaner was obviously the act of someone whose mind had ceased to operate. Still, reflected Sheldon, they might as well go down cleaning.

He followed as The Brain and Helga turned into the control room.

'Stay low,' hissed The Brain to Sheldon, who didn't need reminding. If he'd been any lower, he'd have been sucking carpet. The three of them wriggled past a bright pink creature that bore more than a passing resemblance to the US president, except that it was nude and playing a violin.

The smoke in the room helped mask them from view, but they could see that the SSSU, despite their very best efforts, were losing. Captain Schnurrbart and Agent Frimmel were the only agents left. They stood back to back pouring blast after blast of bullets towards the enemy. Sheldon could see the barrels of both weapons glowing red through the smoke.

Under his feet, Sheldon felt Pandora begin to throb.

The power surge was coming.

With a sickening *click* Captain Schnurrbart ran out of ammunition. Frimmel followed a few seconds later.

A sudden silence descended in the control room and the smoke began to slowly clear. Helga heaved the cleaner upright while The Brain found a power outlet and plugged it in. He hoped that the water from the sprinkler system hadn't short-circuited the power. A glance at the computer screen showed him that the power was still on. He took another lead from his pocket and plugged that into the computer system. Working quickly, he stripped a small section of plastic insulation from the other end of the wire and attached the bare copper to the vacuum cleaner.

'Bravo, Captain,' purred Stokes into the silence. He emerged from behind the bullet-scarred concrete pillar and clapped his hands twice slowly. 'It's fitting that you be here for the final opening.'

He looked at the computer screen.

'In a few seconds Pandora will have a power surge. That will connect with the Duzzent Matter—no matter where you've hidden it—and the multiverse floodgates will open. Everything that's happened up to now will seem like chickenfeed!'

'Shall I multiverse them?' said Number Two with a gesture at Captain Schnurrbart and Frimmel.

'There's no need,' said Stokes. 'Let them watch.'

The platoon of Schnurrbarts stood like automatons around the remaining two SSSU agents, waiting for instructions.

Pandora's power was building up. Everyone in the control room could feel it in their feet, feel it in the steadily building electricity in the atmosphere.

Stokes watched the computer, his eyes glittering with anticipation.

'Not so fast, Stokes!' said The Brain, emerging from

behind a squat mound of dung dropped by some unspecified animal that had appeared in place of agent Vermorel. Helga was pointing the curtain-cleaning hose-attachment from the vacuum cleaner at Stokes.

'And what are you going to do with that, you idiots?' he laughed. 'Hoover me up?'

'Precisely,' said The Brain and pressed the 'on' switch as Pandora's power reached a peak.

This was it.

The vacuum cleaner coughed asthmatically and spluttered into life.

On Stokes's computer screen the power-surge counter ticked down.

Ten seconds. Nine. Eight.

The vacuum cleaner whined.

And nothing happened.

Stokes laughed again. Behind The Brain, Captain Schnurrbart caught Sheldon's eye and made a gesture of defeat. Sheldon wondered if it would be painful when it happened. He wasn't entirely sure what was going to happen when the full force of Duzzent Matter was unleashed, but he knew it probably wouldn't be a good thing.

The reality of the situation was that Helga was pointing the nozzle of a clapped-out vacuum cleaner at a laughing two-headed evil butler, and that they had finally reached the end.

Three seconds. Two. One.

There was a huge pulse of energy that everyone at LURV felt travel through the bottom of their feet right up to the top of their heads. In the case of Stokes, both his heads. He laughed again, but this time Sheldon thought he could detect a note of uncertainty.

Something strange was happening. That much was clear. The walls of the control room seemed to bow inwards and then expand outwards. The floor vibrated with tiny ripples, like a stone dropped in a lake. Was it an earthquake, thought Sheldon? Or was this something bigger, something more universal?

Then a dull boom filled the space around them, as if a jet has passed through the sound barrier, and everyone rocked back on their feet. It happened again and the light inside the control room seemed to thicken.

Pandora, thought Sheldon.

A low buzzing noise filled his ears and, for a microsecond, Sheldon thought he saw every single particle and sub-atomic neutron, electron, quasar and quark in astonishing, blinding clarity. He saw that everything was everything, that everything was made from the same materials: that he was everything and everything was him.

Then he snapped out of it and felt silly, as if he'd been caught reciting poetry at a football game.

In front of him, something was happening to Number Two. He lifted slowly off the floor and, dissolving into glowing particles as he went, drifted towards the vacuum cleaner vibrating in Helga's hands.

'Chief?' said Number One as he began to come apart too. 'Erm, chief?'

Stokes watched, transfixed, his mouth open.

Microscopic piece by microscopic piece, Number One was sucked into the nozzle. With a last, sad look at Stokes, his face disintegrated and he was gone. He was followed by particles and atoms being sucked from the other imitation Schnurrbarts.

Stokes too began to disintegrate. He watched incredulously as his body began to vibrate and then leak towards the nozzle of the vacuum cleaner, feet first.

'No! NO!' he screamed. 'Not now! Not NOW! NOT LIKE THIS!'

Stokes squirmed frantically away from the nozzle, his hands reaching out to hold onto desks, chairs, anything to stop himself being sucked into oblivion. It was useless. Atom by atom the two-headed butler whooshed down the black hole of the vacuum cleaner.

His left head was last to go, snarling as it flowed towards the nozzle.

'I'LL ... BE ... BACK!' he bellowed as his jaw, teeth and lips were sucked up.

The Brain glared directly into his staring eyes as they, too, disappeared. He waggled his fingers as the last of Stokes vanished down the vacuum cleaner tube in mute fury.

'Bye,' said Helga. 'Hasn't been a pleasure, I'm afraid. Don't come again.'

And then he was gone.

34

'Well, that's something you don't see every day,' said Helga.

She lowered the nozzle and stood in the wreckage of the control room, looking at the space where only a few seconds previously, Stokes had been confidently predicting the beginning of a new order: one with him at its centre. Nothing of him remained, not a speck of clothing, not an atom of flesh. It was as if Stokes, Number One, Number Two, and the entire platoon of Schnurrbarts, had never existed.

The Brain sucked thoughtfully on his pipe and clicked the vacuum cleaner's off button. A welcome silence descended on the battle-scarred control room. The vacuum cleaner was not, as Sheldon expected, bulging with whatever was left of the bad guys. Instead it hung down, completely empty.

'Jeez,' said Sheldon, 'that's some cleaner you've got there, Theo.'

Helga looked down the nozzle, half-expecting Stokes to clamber out. 'I had my doubts,' she said. 'But I have to hand it to you, Brain, you called it right.'

Captain Schnurrbart was stunned. His damp moustache was covered in dust, clouds of which also floated around the room, thanks to the high velocity bullets that had ripped great chunks from the plaster walls. He coughed and, like a man emerging from a heavy sleep, stumbled towards the two boys. Behind him, Frimmel—an SSSU agent to his military fingernails—took up a defensive position against any surprise attack.

Sheldon somehow knew there wouldn't be any attack. It was over, whatever 'it' had been. The atmosphere inside LURV felt safer. It was the sort of feeling that reminded Sheldon of the times when he'd had flu for a few days and then, without quite knowing how it had happened, the virus had given up and he instinctively knew that from that point on he'd start getting better.

The Brain leaned towards the computer that had displayed the countdown. He scratched his chin. 'One second left. Cut the thing a little fine,' he said. 'Still the main thing is that it worked, eh?'

'Yes,' said Captain Schnurrbart picking a lump of plaster from his moustache. 'Although I'm still not quite sure *exactly* what happened. Would you care to explain?'

'I'll be happy to do so Captain, in due course. Right now though we still have a little work to do.'

Sheldon's eyes widened. 'Not more fighting? I don't think my ribs could stand it.'

'No,' said The Brain. 'We have to do something about all these things from the other universes.'

As he spoke, the two panthers poked their noses around the door.

'Hey, *amigo*?' said one of them. 'We just heard what you say, man.'

'*Si*,' said the second panther. 'And we were thinking maybe you could get us back to where we came from?'

'If that's not too much trouble, *amigo*?' said the first panther, putting his head on one side in an apologetic manner. At least it looked apologetic. They were panthers after all. There was a limit to the emotions they could show by facial expression.

'Certainly, chaps,' The Brain said.

'All right!' yelled the panthers, giving each other high-fives. 'You the man!'

The Brain moved back towards Pandora's main computer. Although drenched and scarred, it was still in full working order. The Brain sat down and began tapping keys as Captain Schnurrbart and Sheldon gathered round to watch.

'If my theory is right,' said The Brain over his shoulder, 'then it should be a simple matter to instruct Pandora to reverse the Duzzent Matter Event and recover all the people who were hit by the multiversers.'

Sheldon had a sudden thought. Quite an uncomfortable one. 'Um, hold on just a cotton-picking minute, Theo,' he said.

'What is it?' said The Brain, his bony white fingers paused above the keyboard.

'*I* got hit by a multiverser,' said Sheldon.

'Yes?'

'Well, the thing is, how certain are you that this theory of yours will work?'

'Almost entirely,' said The Brain. 'Of course, there is always a slight chance I'm wrong.'

'And if you are wrong? What happens then?'

The Brain scratched his head. 'To be completely honest, I couldn't say for certain.'

'The most likely result,' said Helga, 'is that anyone who'd been hit by a multiverser would be broken down into their constituent atoms and form one homogenous multi-cellular body of semi-liquid carbon.'

'What does that mean?'

'Miss Poom means you'd be turned into soup,' said The Brain.

'Soup?'

Helga smiled sweetly and nodded.

'I do wish you'd stop repeating every last word I say, dear boy,' said The Brain. 'You sound like a parrot. It becomes a trifle tiresome. Yes, soup. But, as I have pointed out, this is not a likely outcome. In fact it has only an eight-point-three percent chance of happening. As you have been returned to your original universe already, nothing whatsoever may happen to you.'

'But . . .'

'Too late,' said The Brain, pressing the 'return' key. 'Pandora has gone to work.'

Everyone looked up as the room shuddered once more and a powerful thrum of electricity filled the air. Sheldon opened his mouth to speak and promptly vanished. The panthers too disappeared. All over the LURV complex, various animals, plants and alien creatures started to vanish, *pop, pop, pop*. The Brain sat back, arms folded, an expression of calm on his pale face. Captain Schnurrbart raised an eyebrow and looked at him quizzically.

'I hope you know what you're doing,' he murmured. 'Have you any idea what my life would be like if Sheldon came home in a bowl? Mrs Schnurrbart would crucify me.'

He rubbed his moustache and glanced round the room as the seconds ticked past. Then, with a soft whoosh of air, Sheldon re-appeared, blinking and nauseous. He coughed once and checked to make sure all parts of his anatomy had arrived back in the same order they'd left. Two legs, two arms, one head, eleven fingers.

'Hey!' shouted Sheldon, holding up his right hand and looking at the extra finger. 'Look!'

'It's an improvement, if you ask me,' muttered Helga. 'Although I suppose it means you could pick up more people's fathers and eat them, too.'

'Oh, well,' said The Brain holding his hands out apologetically. 'Close enough.'

It was a good job the Captain was there, or Sheldon might have done something violent.

35

Over the next few minutes, the rest of the SSSU agents reappeared, all more or less intact. DeKooning did have his nose rather nearer to his mouth than it had been, and Vermorel now sported three ears instead of the regulation two, but, since the third one was only a very small ear and it was underneath Vermorel's left armpit, he didn't kick up too much of a fuss.

Right across the LURV complex, reception staff, maintenance workers, lab technicians, catering staff, office staff, scientists and janitors all popped back into their original forms, wondering exactly what had happened.

Smit, once he'd received attention to his head wound, was in reasonable physical condition, but with webbed fingers. Miss Urtl lost seven kilos in a parallel universe, but she had no complaints about that.

All the students came back safely.

Even the holes in the canteen cheese-sandwiches reappeared.

Professor Weiss and the control-room workers who'd been shrunk to the size of raisins by the Pandora effect, arrived back together with a sudden bang. Professor Weiss's only recognisable change was that his gravelly voice now sounded as though he'd been sucking helium. He looked around at the battle-scarred control room.

'Wh-wha-what happened?' he squeaked.

'Later, Professor,' said Captain Schnurrbart. 'Explanations can wait. Right now I'm going to have to send you down to SSSU to answer some questions.' He nodded to DeKooning. 'Take him away.'

As the SSSU officers began calling in medical assistance, Captain Schnurrbart heard via his radio that Officer Knut had reappeared in place of the blue chicken. He was half-dead with cold and couldn't remember a thing, but he was alive. Captain Schnurrbart felt like opening a bottle of champagne. Instead, he contented himself with smoothing his moustache.

Miss Urtl came into the control room and snapped off a crisp salute.

'Get the school party back home, Officer Urtl,' he said, 'and see to it that they all get a dose of the mind-wipe software before returning them to their parents, understood?'

Urtl nodded. The staff at LURV were of course all so used to keeping quiet about top secret experiments that they could be relied upon to say nothing.

'So, that's everything sorted, then?' said Sheldon leaning back and putting his hands in his pockets. Before anyone could reply, his fingers touched something and he screamed.

'There's something moving in my pocket!' he yelled.

He was right. As everyone looked in horror, Sheldon's pocket began to swell.

'What the ...?' Sheldon began to stagger as whatever was in his pocket grew heavier and heavier. He dropped to his knees as the denim began to rip.

Sheldon screamed as a man dressed in blue overalls rolled out of what was left of his jeans and stood up, blinking uncertainly under the laboratory lights.

The Brain stepped forward.

'*Sind sie Herr Poom? Herr Pieter Poom?*'

The new arrival nodded, his eyes blinking in the light.

'*Ja,*' he said. '*Ich bin Poom. Wo bin ich?*'

'DAD!' screamed Helga and hurled herself at the new arrival. '*DAD!*'

'WHAT?!' Sheldon leaped to his feet. 'Mr *Poom*! What is Helga's dad doing in my pocket?' Sheldon rummaged around in his jeans as if expecting someone else's dad to fall out. He pulled out the lining of his pocket and two lint-covered raisins dropped to the floor.

'They're not . . .?' said Sheldon nervously.

'No, old thing,' said The Brain. 'They're just raisins, I believe. Although I wouldn't recommend eating them.'

Sheldon seriously doubted if he'd ever be able to as much as look at another raisin as long as he lived. Then he realised something. 'Hey! I guess that means I didn't eat him after all!' he said. 'Whoo, hoo!'

He danced around the lab.

'Sheldon,' said The Brain. 'Maybe you should find some new pants before you do any more dancing?'

Helga stopped kissing her father and hugged Sheldon.

'You found him!' she shouted. 'You found him! You wonderful, wonderful boy! You found my father!'

Sheldon beamed. 'I suppose I did, didn't I?' He hugged Helga. 'You know, I think I sort of *knew* I hadn't eaten him.'

Then a nasty thought occurred to him. 'What if I *had*

eaten him?' he said, turning to The Brain. 'Would he have swelled back up inside me?'

The Brain shrugged. 'Almost certainly. Very messy. Hardly bears thinking about.'

Sheldon didn't think he'd ever eat anything again. Although, he supposed, if it meant getting hugged by Helga, he might give it a shot.

All that was left were explanations.

36

'So it turned out that the butler did it?' said Mrs McGlone-Schnurrbart, as she lifted a steaming pot of her experimental fondue to the kitchen counter.

The Brain and Sheldon were sitting on bar stools watching the meal being prepared. In the living room, Helga's father sat in front of the TV, a glass of beer in one hand and a slightly stunned expression on his face. He was watching a show about dancing newsreaders. He smiled the smile of a man who wouldn't understand a single word of the conversation.

'Indeed, my sweet,' said Captain Schnurrbart as he tied a blue-and-white striped apron around his waist. 'A two-headed butler from another universe, but technically, yes, the butler did do it.'

Sheldon dipped a finger in the fondue. He had no intention of tasting it, but he was curious about how it had turned out. Since his mother struggled even with toast, he was keen to see what she'd managed to come up when let loose on a complicated dish like fondue. A small ball of gloop clung to his finger like glue. He shook his hand and the rubbery substance flew across the kitchen, bounced off the chopping board Helga was using and caroomed straight through the open kitchen window like a loose bullet.

'Hey!' said Helga, her eyes full of tears. 'Do you mind?'

'I'm sorry,' said Sheldon. 'I didn't mean to upset you.'

Helga held up the knife. 'Not upset you dolt. Onions.'

'Oh,' said Sheldon. 'Good. I mean ... oh well, you know what I mean.'

The Brain rolled a ball of fondue between his fingers. 'I'm going to pass on the fondue, Mary,' he said. 'I'll stick with the curry if that's alright.'

Mary grabbed a spoon and put a little fondue into her mouth. Her teeth bounced off the rubbery substance and she almost dislocated her jaw. With a sigh, she scraped the rest of it into the bin. 'I don't know why I bother some-times,' she said wearily.

Captain Schnurrbart put his arm around her and kissed her on the cheek. 'Never mind, Mary,' he said. 'Helga looks like she's doing a good job with the curry.'

'You don't mind me cooking, do you, Mrs McGlone-Schnurrbart?' said Helga, poised over the pan.

Mary shook her head. 'You knock yourself out, kid,' she said, reaching for a glass of wine. 'I know my limitations.'

'By the way, Theo,' said the Captain over his shoulder. 'I got a call from Officer Vermorel. He tells me that Professor Weiss is claiming a complete memory loss and, so he says, has no recollection of being involved in any of this.'

'What about the replica Schnurrbarts?' asked The Brain.

'They showed up again ... as moustache hairs. *My* moustache hairs, would you believe! They must have used them to clone the Schnurrbart copies, the *schweins*!'

Helga scraped the onions into a sizzling pan and the unfamiliar aroma of a well-prepared meal spread tanta-lisingly around the kitchen. 'There's only *one* Captain

Schnurrbart,' she said. 'And one Schnurrbart moustache!'

Captain Schnurrbart stroked his moustache protectively and Mary offered him a plate of bhajis Helga had prepared earlier. 'She's right. You're the original, Hans,' she said. 'Have a mushroom bhaji.'

She popped one in her own mouth and then opened her eyes wide.

'What's the matter?' said Helga. 'Too spicy?'

'No,' said Mary. 'The bhaji's fine. It's just those fake Schnurrbarts; you don't think they ever came in *here* do you? Doesn't bear thinking about!'

'I don't think so,' said the Captain. 'Besides, you'd be able to tell the real thing from a fake, wouldn't you Mary?'

'Yeah, yeah, course I would,' said Mary, taking a large sip of wine. 'Course I would.'

The phone rang in the hallway and she went to answer it. 'Back in a tick,' she said, relieved not to have to think anymore about cloned husbands.

Helga wagged her knife at Sheldon and The Brain. 'Are you two just going to sit there all night and watch us cook?'

Sheldon nodded. 'Sounds about right to me,' he said. 'We'd just get in the way. And besides, my ribs hurt too much to do anything useful. I think I'll just sit here and hear The Brain explain everything . . . if he can.'

Sheldon poured a cup of hot chocolate while Helga took a bowl out of a cupboard.

'Would you like something to nibble with that chocolate, Sheldon?' she said. 'My dad got you these.'

Sheldon took the bowl and looked at the contents.

'Raisins,' he said. 'Har har. Very good.'

From the living room, Mr Poom shifted round in his armchair and raised his glass to Sheldon with a broad wink. Sheldon lifted his mug of chocolate to him in a salute and pushed the bowl of raisins away. Helga gave the thumbs up to her father and he turned back to the TV, his shoulders shaking with laughter.

'Get on with it, then,' said Sheldon, taking a noisy slurp of chocolate and looking at The Brain. 'Your moment of glory. You love this bit, don't you?'

'If you mean,' said The Brain sniffily, 'that I enjoyed solving the case, then, yes. This has been a very complicated affair.'

'You're telling me,' said Sheldon who found his head ached every time he tried to piece together the sequence of events. Thankfully the pain in his ribs had subsided a little. It was still painful, but only if he wanted to do anything complicated, like breathing. He took another mouthful of hot chocolate, shifted round on the bar stool and waited.

The Brain looked out of the window at the falling snow. 'As I recollect it was a night very much like this one that Miss Poom asked for our assistance.'

'It was freezing!' agreed Helga. 'And I almost lost my nerve. But isn't it about time you stopped calling me Miss Poom?'

'It was most fortunate you did *not* lose your nerve, Miss ... *Helga*,' said The Brain. 'The search for your father is what led us to LURV. It's terrifying to think what may have happened if you had decided not to call by.'

Captain Schnurrbart slid a rack of naan bread into the oven. 'It was right under our noses all along! I can't believe we didn't spot it sooner.'

'I blame myself, Captain,' said The Brain. 'I had suspicions before Miss Poom's arrival.'

'Suspicions?' asked Sheldon. 'What sort of suspicions?'

'The cheese,' said The Brain.

Sheldon groaned. 'Not the flaming cheese thing!'

'I'm afraid it was "the flaming cheese thing", as you so elegantly put it, Sheldon. As you remember, I noted the mysterious disappearance of the holes in the cheese some days before Miss Poom arrived. It *was* a curiosity that tickled my mind. Disappearing holes are not common, even in something as ordinary as cheese. Therefore the explanation must be an uncommon one, and I wonder if I was a little slow to connect it to LURV. After all, they were researching particles and I was observing something that could be connected with some sort of particle shift. By the way, I checked on the cheese you used in the sandwiches, Mary. It was made from milk produced at Phleminger's farm—the one directly above LURV.'

The Brain kept bouncing the little ball of fondue on the kitchen counter, drew breath and went on. 'When Miss Poom arrived that night, her story about the truck sparked connections in my mind about the LURV project. When she told me that her father had disappeared in the Furcht tunnel, I was immediately alerted to how close that was to LURV.'

'I understand most of that,' said Sheldon, staring into his empty mug. 'I think.'

'Professor Weiss was, in almost all ways, a very clever man—possibly too clever,' said The Brain. 'Weiss, at the helm of LURV, chanced upon one of the most exciting and incredible scientific discoveries in the history of humanity: the multiverse and its link with dark matter. The search for the mysteries of life at the atomic level is one—or was— one of the last great unknowns. I can only imagine Weiss's excitement when Pandora began producing such amazing results!'

'Can you imagine when the panthers first popped out?' said Helga. 'That must have been pretty interesting!'

'And then Stokes arrived,' said Captain Schnurrbart.

'And, as you say, Stokes arrived,' agreed The Brain. 'Stokes was *not* something Weiss had bargained for. Caught up in the thrill of fresh discoveries, Weiss made a crucial mistake. He assumed that *he* was in control of whatever came through the multiverse. Stokes proved how wrong he was. It was a massive error. Stokes had been living life in another universe as some sort of criminal overlord in London—obviously a different, two-headed version of London—when Weiss plucked him out and dumped him in LURV. Not only that, Weiss intended to treat him as an amusing pet, a mere manservant. That was when Stokes decided to get revenge.'

'*Kuck Dir das an, Helga*!' said Helga's father pointing at the screen. '*Monster-LKW-Ralley*!'

'His favourite,' explained Helga. '*Monster Truck Rally*.'

'Hey!' said Sheldon. 'I like that too!' He levered himself off the stool and picked up the bowl of raisins. 'Do you think your dad would like a raisin?'

'Where do you think you're going?' said The Brain. 'This explanation isn't nearly finished.'

'But . . .'

'Never mind "but". Don't you want to hear about your role in saving Mr Poom? That's coming up soon.'

Helga winked at Sheldon. 'My hero!' she mouthed and stirred the pot.

Sheldon almost purred. He sat back down. 'Crack on,' he said, waving his hand magisterially.

'At first,' continued The Brain, 'Stokes lay low, saw how things worked and realised he could never return to the world he'd left. He started to assemble a plan to take over control at LURV and—who knows?—the rest of the planet. His first step was to assemble a platoon of willing helpers based on the Captain Schnurrbart that Stokes had seen visiting LURV previously. The Captain was the perfect model for an army of doppelgangers. It was a relatively simple task for Stokes to create new Schnurrbarts using Pandora's power surges. He made a base for his new army inside the nearby unused bomb shelter complex at the Furcht tunnel.'

'Which is where my father came in,' said Helga.

'Precisely,' said The Brain. 'When Stokes realised that Pandora had produced Duzzent Matter as a by-product of her power surges, he decided to smuggle it to the Furcht to work on in secret. He arranged for a truck company to deliver it to the Furcht. The company was told it was simply a delivery of light bulbs for the complex and that Mr Poom was to take it to a side access road that led almost to Stokes's lair. Unfortunately for your father, his arrival at the destination coincided with a power surge from Pandora. This triggered the Duzzent Matter and it compressed Mr Poom to the size of a . . . raisin.'

Sheldon turned pale. Helga leaned over and patted his arm reassuringly.

'The event also pulled the rocks around the truck, sealing in Mr Poom.'

The oven pinged and Captain Schnurrbart lifted the naan bread out onto a platter. He broke off a piece and popped it into his mouth.

'I suppose,' he said through a mouthful of bread, 'that when Stokes realised that Weiss had produced Duzzent Matter, it was like giving him the keys to the kingdom.'

'That's right,' said The Brain. 'Stokes was the very first to realise that Pandora had produced Duzzent Matter. Not only that, he saw how Duzzent Matter could help him get revenge. At first I think he was only thinking in terms of making Weiss look silly. He wanted LURV to be overcome with silliness and for Weiss to be booted out by the authorities. The Swiss do not like silliness. It is not the Swiss way. But, as he began to hijack Pandora, he began to see how Duzzent Matter could be much, much bigger than he had realised. It didn't take him long to arm his Schnurrbarts with multiversers to—well, you saw what they could do.'

'And the way that they could walk through walls?' said Sheldon. 'What was that about?'

'Particles,' said Helga, 'at a guess.'

The Brain glanced at her.

'Sorry,' said Helga. 'But girls *do* actually have a contribution to make. And I don't just mean making a mean curry.'

The Brain raised his hands in surrender. Captain Schnurrbart suppressed a smile. It wasn't often one saw The Brain knocked flat on his proverbial backside.

'The way I see it,' said Helga waving a chilli-smeared wooden spoon, 'is that Stokes was fiddling with particles. His new Schnurrbarts could, apparently, control their particles so that they could move between the particles of "solid" objects. Stokes hadn't planned on that; it was just an unexpected bonus. Most of an atom is, after all, taken up with "empty" space, right? Solidity is an illusion. Nothing is "rock solid"—at least not at the atomic level. Except perhaps dark matter itself.'

Sheldon shook his head. 'It's that sort of information I find hard to understand,' he said. 'Just give me the bit I need, please!'

'Sheldon, you are a sweet boy, but you really *must* pay more attention. The simple version is that the Schnurrbarts walked through solid objects, much like me or you would wade through water, because they were able to "control" their molecules.'

Captain Schnurrbart leaned forward and dipped a piece of naan bread in the curry.

'Hey!' said Helga and cracked him on the back of his hand with her spoon.

'That is just delicious,' said Captain Schnurrbart, a splash of yellow curry on his moustache. 'Anyway, so Stokes had assembled and armed his "army". And meanwhile Weiss—'

'Yes, Weiss,' said The Brain, hurriedly, taking up the story before Helga could jump in again. 'Weiss began to make plans to unveil his discoveries. Stokes, of course, could not allow that and decided to act.'

Helga winked at Sheldon. 'And Weiss—' she began.

'What Weiss didn't stop to think about,' said The Brain quickly, 'was the fact he was playing with fire. He was so caught up in discovering interesting stuff that he never stopped to think about if it *should* be discovered. But Weiss isn't, I believe, very far removed from Stokes in the madness stakes. He was going to open Pandora wide, let the multiverse run unchecked. Who knows what would have happened?'

'And could he have done that, Theo?' asked Sheldon. 'Seems a bit loony to me.'

'I think he would have succeeded. All the preparations for taking over were almost ready. An army of Schnurrbarts, the creation of the multiverser weapons, which I think were responsible for the—'

'Cuckoo clocks,' interrupted Sheldon. 'That's why those clocks appeared.'

'Exactly. Stokes had them hunted down in case they gave the game away. It almost happened, too. We saw how close the clocks came to escaping that night on the mountain. If they had succeeded, then LURV would surely have been investigated and Stokes's plan would have come to naught. Which is about where we came in.'

'Bravo!' cried Helga. 'That just about does it, right?'

The Brain bowed.

'Credit where it's due,' he said. 'The case only began because we were asked to find Miss Poom's father. And of course it was Sheldon who actually found him!'

Helga leaned across the kitchen counter and gave Sheldon a kiss on the cheek. Sheldon blushed, just as his mother came back into the room with the phone.

'Sean,' she mouthed to Sheldon and pointed at the mouthpiece. 'He says to say "hello". Actually, to be honest, he asked me to give you a dig in the eye with a sharpened pencil, but I knew what he really meant.'

Sheldon waved at the phone and smiled sweetly. 'Tell him I hope his stupid surfboy head falls off and gets eaten by a shark.'

'Sheldon says "hi",' said his mother into the phone. 'Sean! Language! No, I'm not going to tell him that. His girlfriend's here, for one thing.'

'Mum!' said Sheldon.

Helga stifled a laugh.

'No, she's lovely, as a matter of fact, Sean. And no, she does not carry a white stick. And Sean, listen: Sheldon and Theo—yes, the one with the glasses—they've just saved the world or the universe or something, with a vacuum cleaner, and Sheldon rescued Helga's dad when he got turned into a raisin! Didn't they do well?'

Sheldon's mum listened in silence for a moment. It was obvious that Sean had changed the subject. 'They never?' she said, eyes wide. 'Did they? Really? They never did! No! What, twice? *Really?* In full view of everyone? Never!'

Captain Schnurrbart put down the tea towel and gently steered his wife back into the hallway and closed the door. 'That reminds me, Theo,' he said. 'How on earth did you come up with the vacuum cleaner idea? I have to admit that when I saw Helga point it at Stokes I thought you'd gone mad.'

'How do you think I felt?' said Helga. She tasted the curry and kissed her fingers. 'If it hadn't been so serious I'd have burst out laughing.'

'*Gone* mad?' muttered Sheldon. 'What's all this "gone" business? He's been a complete nut job since we first met!'

The Brain ignored their jibes. 'I'd spent enough time with Pandora to realise that her power surges were building towards a Duzzent Matter event,' he said, '*and* that we only had minutes left to do something about it. I knew that if I re-programmed Pandora, it might reverse all the results.'

'And you thought of a vacuum cleaner,' said Sheldon. 'Of course.'

'Yes, Sheldon, I did think of that: a common vacuum cleaner. It was a difficult, almost impossible, piece of programming but I managed to do it. I theorised that if and when Pandora began to reverse the effects of the multiverse, Stokes and the Schnurrbarts might be helpless against a powerful suction. By finding a way to plug the vacuum cleaner into Pandora, I could literally suck them into the cleaner, atom by atom. The very same power that enabled them to pass through seemingly solid materials also made them powerless against a common vacuum cleaner.'

'So I suppose we could have vacuumed them all up earlier?' said Helga.

'Only if we had hooked up the vacuum cleaner to Pandora,' said The Brain. 'But yes, that would have been possible, in theory.'

Mrs McGlone-Schnurrbart wandered phoneless back into

the room and patted her stomach. 'Wow, that smells good!' she said, sniffing the air. 'I don't know about anyone else, but I've had about all the explaining I can take for one day. I'm *hungry*. I just need to know one thing before we eat.'

'Yes?' said The Brain.

'Are you quite *sure* this is the real Captain Schnurrbart?'

There was an awkward pause during which the Captain's moustache twitched. Then he lurched towards his wife with a strange, faraway look in his eyes, his hands extended, claw-like and stiff. Mary and Helga backed away in terror. Mr Poom got uncertainly to his feet.

'Must. Kill. Humans.' Schnurrbart's voice was strained, menacing. 'MUST. KILL. HUMANS!'

Sheldon leapt off the bar stool, his heart bouncing around in his chest. 'For God's sake, Theo!' he yelled. '*Do* something!'

The Brain pointed to the cupboard under the stairs. 'Get the vacuum cleaner, Sheldon! Quick!'

Sheldon raced across the room as Schnurrbart advanced zombie-like towards Mary. With fumbling hands, Sheldon wrenched open the door of the cupboard and dragged the cleaner out. He scrambled the plug into the electrical socket and whirled round, nozzle in one hand and cleaner in the other, to find everyone laughing hysterically.

'Very funny,' he said and threw the vacuum cleaner at them.

37

The food had been eaten, the stories told, and now only Sheldon and Helga remained awake. Sheldon didn't know exactly why, but he had a jittery feeling in his stomach.

Probably the curry, he figured.

The trouble was, he spent large chunks of time wanting to be alone with Helga, but when it finally happened, like *now*, he didn't know what to do.

Girls were complicated.

Shouldn't there be a manual he could check? A set of instructions?

He picked up the remote control and thought about watching TV. Then some basic instinct told him that watching repeats of *Monster Truck Rally* when alone with a girl was, almost certainly, a big no-no. He dropped the remote.

The pause was threatening to tick over into a full-blown awkward moment. Sheldon searched for something, anything, to fill the gap.

'More chocolate?' he said, walking over to the kettle.

Helga laughed. 'You're *addicted!* You must have a couple of litres swilling around inside. But yes, why not?'

Grateful for something to do, Sheldon busied himself making drinks. He poured out two mugs and walked across to where Helga was looking out of the window. With a nod of thanks, Helga took hers, opened the door to the deck and stepped out into the snow drifting down from the night sky.

Sheldon was confused again. What was she doing going out into the snow? Should he go too, or did she want to be alone?

After hesitating for a moment like a nervous base jumper on the edge of a high-rise building, Sheldon shrugged himself into a warmer jumper and followed her outside, his feet crunching softly in the snow.

'Aren't you cold?' he asked, wrapping his hands around the mug and watching the flakes of snow dissolve with a hiss on the surface of the chocolate.

'Absolutely freezing,' said Helga, 'but the air feels good after a night inside, doesn't it?'

'I guess so,' said Sheldon.

But he was thinking: what does she want me to do?

Then with a flash he realised what it was. He darted back inside, re-appearing triumphantly a few moments later with a ski jacket.

'Here,' he said, draping it around Helga's shoulders. 'That should do the trick.'

'Er, thanks,' she said. 'But you do have a lot to learn about girls, don't you?'

She was dead right about that. The ski jacket had seemed like a good idea. But obviously it hadn't hit the target. Sheldon figured that understanding exactly what he was supposed to do in this situation seemed as distant a possibility as understanding, well, particle physics.

'Um, yeah, I guess,' he said. 'Don't you want the coat?'

Helga put her head on one side and looked at him in the light from the street lamp.

'The coat's fine. Thanks. It's just that when someone's alone with a girl—in the *moonlight*, I should point out, although I suppose that, technically there's no actual moon out tonight, but you know what I mean—and that someone has been something of a hero to the girl, and then the girl tells the hero she's cold ... the girl is probably *not* asking the hero to go and fetch a coat!'

'Oh,' said Sheldon. 'Right. Isn't she? I mean, aren't you? Isn't he? Sorry, I didn't follow all that.'

'What I mean, *idiot*, is that the girl wants someone to warm her up another way. Like, for instance putting his arms around her.'

'Oh,' said Sheldon again.

There was a short silence.

'And you're the girl, yeah?'

'Of course I'm the girl!'

'Right. Got it. I understand now. I think.'

'So?' said Helga setting her cup of chocolate down in the snow on the railing.

Sheldon looked at her uncertainly.

'Oh, for goodness sake, Sheldon!' said Helga and pulled his arms towards her.

Sheldon found himself hugging Helga.

It felt nice.

And she was hugging him.

They were hugging.

'That's better,' said Helga, 'isn't it?'

'Mm, yeah, mm, much better,' said Sheldon. 'Lot warmer.'

He looked down at her and smiled nervously.

'Now what?' he said. 'This is great and all, but I just want to make sure I don't do anything else wrong.'

Helga tilted her face towards his. 'Nothing can go wrong now,' she whispered.

With a jolt that almost blew him out of his boots, Sheldon realised that she was going to kiss him.

Omigod.

The technical difficulties alone seemed almost too much to bear. What about nose alignment? Teeth clash? Did his breath smell of stale chocolate? Lips—open or closed?

There was no time to think all the answers through. The kiss was happening, right there, right then.

Sheldon angled his head one way. That didn't seem right, so he turned it the opposite way. Better. At least his mouth seemed to be heading in the right direction. Houston, we are go for docking. Helga closed her eyes and slowly moved her head forward. Sheldon puckered his lips.

This was it, he thought.

Which was when, out of the corner of his eye, Sheldon noticed something. A snowflake had landed on Helga's hair.

A pink snowflake.

Then he looked up and saw, with astonishment, that the sky was full of bright pink snow.

Helga opened her eyes and looked at Sheldon, her lips set to 'kiss' mode. 'What are you *doing*?' she hissed.

'Look!' he said, letting go of her and pointing to the sky. '*Pink* snow! This looks serious.'

He dashed inside the house. 'Theo,' he shouted. 'Theo, wake up! You got to see this!'

Sheldon had reached the door before he realised what he'd done.

He froze.

Behind him—he didn't dare turn round to check—he sensed Helga's eyes burning a great smouldering hole in his back. And he knew, just *knew*, pink snow or no pink snow, that he'd absolutely, totally, one hundred percent, blown The Big Kiss.

Sheldon groaned softly and leaned his head against the door frame. Very deliberately, he knocked his forehead against the hard, cold wood.

Then he did it again.

And again.

He found it helped.